"You're hell-bent on coaxing me to be profiled,"

Piers said.

"You could say that," Suzy agreed guardedly.

"The way you were hell-bent on coaxing me once before?" Piers inquired in a soft menacing tone. "The way you seduced me into doing something that I had strong doubts about, but which *you* very much desired?"

Memories ricocheted through her mind and a hot wave of color flooded up her throat. How could she ever have been so shameless?

ELIZABETH OLDFIELD's writing career started as a teenage hobby, when she had articles published. However, on her marriage the creative instinct was diverted into the production of a daughter and son. A decade later, when her husband's job took them to Singapore, she resumed writing and had her first romance accepted in 1982. Now hooked on the genre, she produces an average of three books a year. They live in London, and Elizabeth travels widely to authenticate the background of her books.

Books by Elizabeth Oldfield

ELIZABETH OLDFIELD

Love's Prisoner

Harlequin Books

TORONTO • NEW YORK • LONDON
AMSTERDAM • PARIS • SYDNEY • HAMBURG
STOCKHOLM • ATHENS • TOKYO • MILAN
MADRID • WARSAW • BUDAPEST • AUCKLAND

ISBN 0-373-11773-6

LOVE'S PRISONER

First North American Publication 1995.

CHAPTER ONE

SUZY set her knife and fork back down on her plate with an unsteady clatter. 'You want me to include Piers Armstrong in my book?' she enquired.

The portly middle-aged man who sat on the other side of the lunch table nodded. 'If you do, sales will skyrocket.'

'But you've already accepted the manuscript,' she protested, her voice gathering up an edge of panic, 'and the publication date has been arranged!'

'That's no problem. We can shove it forward by a couple of months,' Randolph Gardener, editorial director of the Kingdom Publishing Company, told her, in jovial reassurance. 'Armstrong's unexpected release is a fantastic stroke of luck for you,' he went on. 'Of all the poor devils who've been held hostage of late, he's the one who seems to have most gripped the public's imagination, so he's the chappie everyone will hand over their hard-earned cash to read about.'

Suzy frowned down at her prawn and mango salad which, with the seafood arced in a succulent pink fan and the fruit sliced into juicy golden leaves, was presented *nouvelle cuisine* style. Ever since the invitation had been issued a few days ago she had been looking forward to lunching here, at one of London's most exclusive and élite French restaurants, but all of a sudden her appetite had disappeared. Vanished. She had envisaged receiving praise for a job well done, not being hit with a demand which was provoking an uncharacteristic yet none the less loud-hailing anxiety attack. Piers Armstrong's release last month came as a personal name-tagged gift from heaven? Not in her opinion. While she had naturally been relieved when, after a year of being held captive by Central American guerrillas, he and his fellow hostage, a US photographer, had been freed, Suzy now wished she had worked faster on her book so that its processing could have safely, *incontrovertibly* passed the point of no return. She wished Randolph had not been able to identify what he apparently regarded as a wondrous window of opportunity.

'My contract specified a hundred and fifty thousand words, so if Piers Armstrong is featured it means one of the other profiles will need to be dropped,' she said, clamping down on her alarm and striving to sound unemotional and matter-of-fact. 'That isn't fair. Each of the men I interviewed very generously gave up several days of their time, and——'

'No one will be dropped, because we shall be increasing the length of the book,' Randolph informed her. He tasted his wine, rhapsodised knowingly on its excellence, then leant across to pat her hand with pudgy fingers. 'I realise what a nuisance it is to have to yank yourself up by your bootstraps, get the adrenalin flowing again and produce another slug just when it seemed you could relax, but once the royalty cheques start to appear you'll be the first to agree that the effort was well worth while,' he said, speaking in the kind of soothing tones which air hostesses adopted to pacify passengers during turbulence.

Suzy took a sip of spa water. The royalties would be her major source of income over the next year or two and thus the amount she received was important, yet even so . . .

'You were happy with my book as it stood,' she said, her chin taking on a stubborn slant.

'We were delighted,' her host acknowledged, 'and we would have been delighted to have gone ahead and published it as it stood—*if* Armstrong hadn't suddenly resurfaced. However, my board and I feel the chance to include him is one which can't be missed.' He slid her a baited smile. 'And now we're also thinking of following the hardback edition with a paperback.'

Joy burst inside her like fireworks. A paperback would mean a far wider readership and could help lodge her name in the public consciousness. It would also vastly increase her royalties. Suzy battened down her joy. She refused to be lured.

'I don't see that Piers Armstrong's insertion would make that much of a difference,' she insisted.

Randolph heaved a sigh. After spending well over a year on research and writing, her reluctance to tackle an additional case history was only natural, yet he had felt certain that any hesitation would be brief and easily overridden. In all their previous dealings Suzy Collier had shown herself to be open to ideas and co-operative, so why must she be contrary now?

'It'll make a vast difference,' he insisted. 'You see, while the other men you've profiled are each of interest in their own way, none is a formidably tough war correspondent. Neither are any of them tall, dark and handsome.'

'That matters?' she protested.

'It'll be a tremendous plus point in marketing. Selling books is just like selling any other commodity, in that if you can identify an aspect which'll spice up the consumer's interest you go all out to promote it.'

Suzy speared a prawn. 'I don't consider Piers Armstrong handsome,' she said. 'He may have beautiful eyes—pale grey and fringed with thick black lashes—but his face is too angular, his nose too hawklike, his jaw too blunt.'

'Sounds as though you've studied the chappie in some detail,' her companion observed, plastering a finger of toast with his favourite goose liver pâté.

The heat seeped into her cheeks. 'I—I used to know him,' she muttered.

'Of course, you once worked on *The View* too—I'd forgotten. Well, even if Armstrong isn't perfect feature by feature, the public—with an emphasis on the female variety—regard him as something akin to a film star, and if what you write could be illustrated by a few photographs of the fellow looking hunky, as my adolescent daughter calls it——' Randolph guffawed '—you'd be guaranteed the number one slot on the non-fiction bestsellers list.'

Suzy bit into the prawn with sharp white teeth. The editorial director was fantasising. She knew enough about popular taste to know she had not the least hope of toppling the ubiquitous epistles on diets or keep fit or cookery; though that was not her aim. All she really aspired to for this, her first book, was decent crits and respectably encouraging sales. At twenty-six, she was only starting to climb the literary ladder of success. In any case, whatever their appeal, returned hostages were nine-day wonders, and by the time her work reached the shelves next spring the hullabaloo which Piers Armstrong's release had created would be long over. As their liaison was long over, she thought, and her face clouded. Whether the war correspondent's inclusion in her book could be construed as an asset or not, there was another reason— a significant and personal reason—why she rebelled against writing about him, but she felt disinclined to say this to someone who was no more than an acquaintance, and who could proceed to ask probing questions.

'Didn't you once mention knowing Armstrong's father, the famous Hugo?' Randolph recalled, as he munched.

Tall and patrician, with silver-white hair, Hugo Armstrong was a distinguished actor and occasional director, a man of considerable clout in the theatrical world.

Suzy gave a distracted nod. 'I interviewed him for an article about stage trends in the nineties a month or so before his son disappeared, and we've kept in touch. Piers may not want to relive his experiences,' she went on, doggedly pushing out another impediment.

'Since his return a hundred and one reporters must have asked him about them, and he's always obliged,' Randolph retorted.

'But he hasn't been interviewed in depth, for a book.'

'Everyone else who's been approached has jumped at the chance of question-and-answer sessions with a pretty girl like you and, particularly as a one-time colleague, Armstrong will too,' the editorial director asserted.

Suzy started to object, decided otherwise, and returned to her prawn and mango salad.

Randolph had already demolished his first course, and as she ate he poured himself a second glass of wine and subjected her to a covert scrutiny. His reference to her as 'pretty' had been a calculated ploy to cajole, yet he had been speaking the truth. With huge sapphire eyes, fine bone-structure and a soft, full mouth, the youngest writer on Kingdom's list was quite a beauty. She also possessed a natural sexuality which, although she seemed unaware of it, had ensured that when they had walked into the restaurant every male had turned to drool over her—and to envy him. Were they under the impression that this slender creature in the pink linen suit and with her wheat-blonde tresses caught up in a sleek chignon might be his mistress? he wondered. Randolph sneaked a glance at the surrounding tables. It was flattering to think so. He *hoped* so. A wistful hand checked over his carefully cross-combed bald patch. If only he were twenty years younger, twenty-eight pounds lighter, and still in possession of a full head of hair.

'As you'll probably be aware, after the airport press conference Armstrong was whisked straight off to the Margaux Clinic for a thorough medical overhaul,' Randolph continued, topping up his glass. 'Yesterday I telephoned the clinic and although I was unable to speak to the chappie in person, the reply came back that he's willing to see you.'

Suzy's blue eyes opened wide. 'You've made an appointment?' she said, in horror.

'For later this afternoon,' came the smiling confirmation.

'But—but Piers is still recovering,' she protested.

'Maybe, yet he's agreed to a visit. So you can pop along when we've finished lunch and set up a series of meetings.'

Suzy felt at once knocked askew and annoyed. Renewing contact with Piers Armstrong had never featured in her scheme of things and she resented the editorial director's taking it upon himself to organise so high-handedly without consulting her.

'I have an appointment for later this afternoon,' she said.

Randolph tweaked at the white damask napkin which covered his lap. The girl's beauty came accompanied by a full complement of brains, so why couldn't she see that, whatever the hassle, the insertion of the war correspondent into her book was entirely to her advantage? Why wasn't she grabbing this chance to dramatically boost her sales—and Kingdom's profits—with both hands? A swift untasted drink was quaffed from his glass. He had sat down at the table in the expectation of wining and dining a biddable young companion who would hang on his every word, and he did not appreciate becoming embroiled in an argument which was threatening to ruin his digestion.

'What time is your appointment, and where?' he demanded, sounding like an irked schoolmaster.

'Four-thirty, in Fulham.'

'I've fixed for you to be at the clinic some time after three o'clock,' he said, as a waiter removed their empty plates and replaced them with *boeuf en croûte*

à la reine Marie for him and lemon sole for his guest.
'It can be no more than a ten-minute taxi ride from
here, so you have ample opportunity to call in and
speak to Armstrong first.'

Suzy frowned. 'Even so——'

'The deadline for your manuscript may have been
extended by eight weeks, but time is of the essence,'
he snapped.

Suzy helped herself to *mange-touts* from a dish
which the waiter had proffered. It was clear that her
host's patience was fast running out and if she continued to protest she would not only sour their lunch
date, but could place any future goodwill at risk—
which would be short-sighted and counter-productive.
Kingdom were a major company in the publishing
world, and it would be foolish to offend them.

'I'll see Piers Armstrong today,' she said resignedly.

Randolph beamed. 'That's a good girl,' he said,
and, after reaching across to give her hand another
pat, he contentedly devoted himself to his fillet in its
filo pastry case.

As directed, Suzy took the lift to the third floor and
turned right on to a broad pastel-walled corridor. She
checked her watch. Having secured her agreement to
visit the private hospital, Randolph Gardener had
proceeded to spend the rest of the meal chatting
amiably and volubly, and—perhaps due to an over-
indulgent intake of wine—had seemed immune to how
the afternoon had begun to tick away. In the end, she
had been forced to make her apologies and leave him
still savouring a liqueur. On emerging on to the street,
she had taken ages to find a taxi, and then the vehicle

had travelled barely a mile before becoming snarled up in a traffic jam. So now time really *was* of the essence.

Still, her visit would not take long, Suzy comforted herself, as she kept track of the numbers on the pale oak doors. She was only here to pacify Randolph and go through the motions. Lacklustre motions. Her request for interviews would be so apathetic that Piers Armstrong would be certain to demur; at which point she would be out of the clinic—fast. A line etched itself between her brows. It was possible that this distaste for a collaboration could be two-sided and the ex-hostage might harbour misgivings of his own—but if that was the case, it would make securing his refusal so much easier.

Piers must have been surprised to be told that Suzy Collier required an audience, she reflected, standing aside to allow a porter with a trolley pass by. Though it would not have thrown him, and his equilibrium would not have been shattered. Randolph's request might have made it annoyingly apparent that the war correspondent still possessed the power to unsettle her, but she would have been dismissed as no more than a blip in his sexual history long ago. Indeed, he had probably forgotten all about her.

Suzy's heels rapped out a brisk staccato on the tiled floor. If Piers Armstrong had wiped her from his memory, she had not spent the past few years thinking about him—no, sirree! On the dénouement of their liaison, the 'career woman' button had been determinedly pushed, and the responsibilities and pressures which had resulted had left her little time to brood. Those responsibilities and pressures had also made her grow up. The girl who had once been far too gullible, far too naïve—as brutally demonstrated by her brush with the journalist—had matured into a poised and aware young woman. A young woman who was now nobody's fool.

Suzy's march came to a halt. Here was the specified room. She neatened the line of her cropped jacket and smoothed the high-waisted skirt over her hips. Opening her clutch bag, she found a mirror and tidied her hair. A slick of rosy lipstick was applied. She stared at her reflection. Don't look so frightened, so tense, so agitated! she instructed herself. He can't hurt you now.

Raising a hand, she rapped on the door.

'Come in,' said a deep melodious voice which, even after all this time, seemed woefully familiar.

Her stomach churned and she felt a strong impulse to turn tail and run. What was she doing here? Suzy wondered. Why had she allowed herself to be steamrollered into calling on Piers Armstrong? She should have vetoed the suggestion of adding a section on him point-blank. She ought to have insisted that, as it had been accepted and fulfilled the terms of the contract, her book must be published, as was. Though could she do that? The small print would need to be checked.

'Come in,' the voice commanded again, a touch impatiently this time.

Suzy straightened her shoulders, summoned up a smile, and strode into a functional but comfortable magnolia-painted room made airy by a large picture window. A man with thick dark hair was sitting on the edge of a quilt-covered bed, idly leafing through a newspaper. In an open-throated midnight-blue shirt, black Levis and suede desert boots, no concession had been made to the fact that he was a patient. Her nerve-ends corkscrewed. Piers Armstrong had always dressed casually, and yet there was something in the way he held his body, in his personal dynamic, which imparted an aura of masculine elegance to the simplest of shirts and jeans. In the past, she had found this most appealing, and it registered that she still did. Her smile became a little strained.

'Good afternoon,' she said.

Piers rose to his feet. 'Long time no see,' he remarked drily.

Although she had watched his return on the television news, confronting him in the flesh was entirely different. His face looked thinner, the skin was stretched taut over his high cheekbones, and the crinkle lines at the corners of his eyes were deeper. When she had known him before, his hair had been cut short, but now the silky brown-black waves brushed against his shirt collar. Add a tan which he had picked up from somewhere, and Piers Armstrong looked darkly feral and romantic, like a modern-day pirate.

To her dismay, Suzy felt a catch form in her throat. When she had seen him on television she had wept, for his father's sake and out of normal sensitivity to his plight, but—oh, heavens!—she must not weep now. Piers might misinterpret her tears and think she was crying over him as *him*, rather than over him as a returned hostage. She swallowed hard, twice. An innate sentimental streak meant that she would have been tempted to cry when faced with *any* person in his position, Suzy assured herself.

'Yes, it must be——' she paused, pretending to pin-point a date which had been engraved in capitals on her heart '—three years since we last met.' For a moment she wondered whether she ought to indicate the formality of her visit by shaking his hand, but decided against it. Infantile though it seemed, the prospect of even such run-of-the-mill physical contact was disturbing. 'How are you?' she asked.

'Fine.' His pale grey eyes travelled from the top of her blonde head, down the curves of her body, to her high-heeled sandals in a leisurely but all-encompassing appraisal. 'You're looking well. Very much the classy lady in the power suit.'

Suzy shot him a glance from beneath her lashes. Was that a compliment, or a dig at the change he must see in her? It was not only her character which had matured, but also her looks and her dress sense.

'I've been out to lunch,' she said, by way of explanation.

Piers gestured towards a chintz-covered armchair which, together with a small sofa and occasional table, formed a sitting area for visitors.

'Have a seat.'

'Thanks. So—you're coming through your medical tests with flying colours?' Suzy enquired, in a bright, conversational voice.

Although her stay would be as short as possible, she needed to comment on his situation. Indeed, after listening to the other hostages' tales, she was well aware of how at a loss and disorientated Piers must be feeling and, as a caring human being, she sympathised.

He nodded. 'The doctor's verdict is that I'm in good working order,' he said, and, as if to demonstrate, he flexed his shoulders.

'You appear to be more muscular than I remember,' Suzy remarked, her eyes drawn to the contours beneath the deep blue shirt.

'Every time my captors untied me I made a point of doing press-ups and sit-ups,' Piers explained, 'so although I've never been puny I'm in better shape now than I've ever been.' A dark brow arched. 'You'd really see a difference if you saw me stripped.'

Her cheeks pinkened. Why had she commented on his physique? she wondered. It had been a mistake. The last thing she wanted was to revive memories—of how she had seen Piers stripped; of how, also, naked, she had been held against his chest; of how they had once been lovers.

'I don't want to take up too much of your time,' she began, primly switching into the work mode.

He strolled over to lounge a broad shoulder beside the window. 'You may take all the time you wish,' he said, gazing outside at the big city panorama of roofs and towering office blocks. 'Anything to relieve the monotony and make the afternoon pass quicker.'

Suzy's lips compressed. A man whose career had had him constantly moving from one trouble spot of the world to another, Piers Armstrong possessed a low boredom threshold—as she knew to her cost, she thought astringently. It was obvious that he would be chafing against being confined to the clinic; as he would have chafed against being held hostage. But while she had not been exactly falling over herself to see him, she objected to being informed that all she

represented was a better-than-nothing diversion who
had been granted admittance into his presence simply
because he was fed-up!

'Pity I didn't bring some tiddlywinks, then we could
have had a game,' she said, a touch tartly.

His mouth tweaked. 'It would have put a hell of a
kick into my afternoon.'

'When are you due to be discharged?' she asked.

'At the weekend, and it can't come soon enough,'
Piers said, with feeling. 'But to what do I owe the
pleasure of this visit?'

Suzy looked at him in surprise. 'You don't know?'

'I was in the middle of some tests when the recep-
tionist rang to say you wished for a pow-wow, so I
couldn't ask.' He thrust her a sardonic look.
'However, I doubt if you're here merely to enquire
about the state of my health.'

'I've come to ask if you'd agree to—to my interviewing you,' Suzy said, the need to ask *him* for a
favour, albeit one she did not want, making it difficult to prise the words from her throat. 'Though if
you're sick and tired of speaking to people, I shall
understand,' she added, at speed.

Piers' brow furrowed. 'You want to interview me
for the *Pennant*?' he enquired, referring to the newspaper which she had worked for after she had left *The
View*—and broken with him. 'But I've already spoken
to a man from there.'

'No, I left them over twelve months ago, and now
I'm writing a book for Kingdom Publishing on the
worldwide hostage scene,' she told him. 'It includes
a number of case histories which detail how people
have reacted to being kidnapped and the effect it's

had on their feelings, their beliefs and their lives, with an accent on the human/family side. What I require are some sessions which would enable me to compile a similar case history on you. However, I——

Piers snapped upright. 'You're jumping on the bandwagon of my being held hostage too?' he demanded, his voice as rat-a-tat as a terrorist's machine-gun.

Suzy recoiled, taken aback both by the unexpected accusation and by the force of his hostility.

'I'd simply be doing a job,' she protested.

'You're another rip-off merchant, another opportunist,' he grated, and gave a bleak scornful laugh. 'I should have known!'

She recognised this as an allusion to the past, and her chin lifted.

'It's Kingdom's idea that you should be featured in the book, not mine,' she told him. 'And it was Randolph Gardener, their editorial director, who rang to fix an appointment for this afternoon—rang to fix it *without* my knowledge.'

Piers studied her through narrowed eyes. 'After having already been asked to endorse such things as a security system and a hamburger——'

'A hamburger?' she echoed, in astonishment.

'Crazy, isn't it? I'm well aware that there are those who perceive me solely as a commercial proposition,' he continued, 'so presumably Kingdom are eager to include me because they believe my name in the blurb will pump up sales?'

'Well . . . yes,' Suzy admitted, wishing he was not so astute.

While they had been speaking, she had undertaken a swift assessment. Not only was Piers Armstrong in good physical shape, he seemed mentally sturdy, too. At a loss? Disorientated? No way. All the other ex-hostages she had met had been psychologically scarred by their experiences and, while his year of captivity had been shorter than some, she had assumed that he too would be altered. Maybe a touch diffident, maybe less certain. The assumption was incorrect. Her erst-while lover had always been magnificently secure, and he continued to exhibit an indomitable self-assurance. His ordeal appeared to have already been worked through and set aside, which, Suzy decided, must be because his often dangerous career had made him better able than most to cope with stress.

'So you're here because of the fistful of dollars factor,' he said, his lip twisting in derision.

'Personally I couldn't care less about any extra money which your inclusion may or may not gen-erate,' she replied. 'And,' she added, feeling com-pelled to make it clear that any influence he might have once had over her had long since disappeared, 'the book was started before you were kidnapped, so I had absolutely no reason to think that there would ever be any need to write about you.'

Piers' shirtsleeves were rolled up above his elbows and he began to re-roll one which was coming loose. 'Why choose hostages as your subject?' he enquired.

'I didn't, it was chosen for me,' said Suzy, watching the movements of his tapered fingers as he tightened the blue cotton over the smooth brown muscle of his arm. 'When I worked at the *Pennant* I was assigned to cover the return of first one man and then another who'd been taken captive. Randolph Gardener happened to read my articles, liked them, and contacted me to ask whether I'd be interested in a commission to write a book. As I was growing weary of being sent haring off around the country at a moment's notice, it seemed like a good idea. Even though it meant giving up a decent salary,' she added, determined to show he could not pin the charge of 'gold-digger' on her.

'So how do you manage?' Piers asked.

'By living off my savings and the interest on some money which my grandmother left me, plus I sell the occasional freelance article and do a regular monthly piece for the *Pennant*.'

'What kind of a piece?'

'Something which offers a fresh angle on a topical news event, either at home or abroad. With regard to my book,' Suzy went on, deciding she had better say a little more about it, just in case Randolph Gardener should ask, 'I've done five profiles, so far. One features a French businessman who——'

'Was held for a million-dollar ransom in a cave in the Dordogne,' said Piers.

'That's right. You remember him?'

'I do.' Pale grey eyes snared hers. 'However, while I've no doubt the guy must have been overjoyed to merit inclusion in your tome,' he drawled, 'there's no way I would ever agree to *you* writing about *me*.'

Suzy's lips thinned. Engineering his refusal was one thing, being given such a blunt and disdainful thumbs-down was another. She could understand him having one or two misgivings, but there was no justification for him to be so unflatteringly, demeaningly, over-whelmingly *anti*.

'You don't think I'd make a decent job of it?' she demanded. 'I may have done women's page stuff when I was with *The View*, but if you'd read anything I produced at the *Pennant* you'd know that when I moved on there I moved into serious reportage.'

A brow lifted. 'You don't say?'

'I do,' Suzy shot back, piqued to think that knowing her must have had so little impact that, once they had split, Piers had never bothered to read anything she had subsequently written. 'Do you imagine Randolph Gardener would have given me the commission if I'd been going to scribble away at the soap opera level? No chance. He reckons I have an instinctive perception which has nothing to do with age or experience, plus I'm diligent and tenacious. Maybe I have yet to rise to the heady heights of winning awards like you, but I can assure you that my appraisal of the hostage situation is intelligent, sober and well crafted,' she informed him fiercely.

'Congratulations,' said Piers with such a mocking bow of his head that she felt an acute urge to hit him. 'However, your writing skills are not the issue.'

'No?' she said dubiously.

'No,' he replied.

Suzy inspected her watch. The minutes were galloping by, but before she left she needed to know why he was so averse to being included in her book. It would be a book of some value, dammit!

'You're anxious to be off?' he enquired.

'I have to be in Fulham in half an hour,' she told him.

'What's happening there?'

'I have appointments to view a couple of flats. Look, about——'

'You're leaving your place in Putney?'

Suzy gave a brief nod. 'About——'

'Why?' Piers asked, interrupting again.

'The house has been sold to someone who wants to turn it back into a family home, so I'm under notice to quit.' She sighed. 'I'd found somewhere else and thought everything was settled, but at the last moment the rent was increased and I couldn't afford it.'

'When's your deadline for moving out?'

'Two weeks today. I've been dashing around looking at all kinds of places, but I've acquired a few goods and chattels——'

'I remember your home-making streak,' Piers muttered.

'—and finding furnished accommodation with sufficient space to take everything *and* which is in my price range isn't easy.'

He strolled back over to the window. 'You aren't in the market for shacking up with a boyfriend?' he enquired.

Suzy shook her head. 'No.'

Piers slid his hands into the hip pockets of his denims and rested his shoulders back against the wall, a position which contrived to thrust forward his pelvis.

'Gone prissy in your old age?' he asked.

She recognised the query as the gibe he intended.

'It isn't a question of that,' she replied.

'You don't have a boyfriend?'

'I do,' Suzy said quickly.

His question had sounded like a challenge, and to admit to the truth—that she was presently unattached—would have seemed like an admission of failure.

'The man doesn't have enough room for you and your possessions?' Piers enquired.

''Fraid not,' she said, wishing he would not stand in a way which had made her aware of the zippered crotch of his jeans and the male outline beneath the stretched denim. In a way which was making her feel short of breath and . . . distracted.

'What's your boyfriend called?' he asked.

'Um——' she searched for a name '—Jo.'

'Jo what?'

'Manning.'

She did have a friend called Jo Manning, but the 'Jo' was short for Joanna.

'What does he do for a living?'

'Works in an investment bank,' Suzy said, hastily transferring facts which related to the female accountant to the make-believe boyfriend.

'If you can't find suitable accommodation in the next fortnight, what happens then?' asked Piers.

'My parents suggested I move back in with them for a while, but Dorset is too far away.' She grimaced. 'So——'

'How are your parents?' he cut in.

'They're very well, thanks. So,' Suzy continued, 'I'll need to put my bits and pieces into store and seek temporary asylum with a girl friend, but storage is costly, and if I stay with——' she almost said with Jo '—with someone, it'll mean sleeping on a sofa. You're reluctant to be interviewed because you think it'll interfere with your plans to visit people, to take a holiday?' she hazarded, executing an abrupt change of tack. 'It won't. I'll fit in with whatever——'

'I'm not going anywhere,' he said. 'My editor's forbidden me from returning to work for at least another month——' he frowned '—much to my disgust, but I intend to stay at home.'

Her sapphire-blue eyes stretched wide. 'You're spending the next four weeks at your apartment in Barnes?' she protested, astonished that a man who had once thrived on travelling, and who had so recently been confined, should display such an uncharacteristic lack of wanderlust.

'Why shouldn't I?' he enquired.

'Well, I'd have thought that——'

Suzy stopped short as his reason for staying home suddenly hit. After a year away, Piers would want time, peace and quiet in which to re-establish his relationship with Amanda Dundas, the actress—and doubtless to express his gratitude. She gave a silent cryptic laugh. When he'd disappeared, his father had immediately launched a campaign to keep Piers' plight in the public eye and try to secure his release. Hugo Armstrong had written to innumerable governments, paid endless calls on politicians, chivvied his theatrical associates into taking part in regular 'support the hostage' events which he had organised. Among those roped in had been Amanda. The reed-slim brunette had taken a part in a play-reading which had attracted nationwide publicity, and subsequently issued a press statement saying how devoted she had been to Piers, how much she missed him, and how she hoped everyone would work towards his freedom.

The implication was that her own efforts were and would continue to be unstinting.

It had not been so. While Amanda had rushed to give newspaper and TV interviews, when she'd contrived to look both melancholy and yet incredibly fetching, she had avoided any common-or-garden slog. Other people—Suzy included—might have performed office duties, walked miles putting up posters, sold tickets and programmes *ad infinitum*, but Piers' girlfriend had done nothing. However, this had not stopped her from turning up at the airport on his return and throwing herself sobbing into his arms; though it had been noticeable that the sobs had not been hard enough to make her mascara run or her eyes go puffy. And at the press conference which followed, she had given a shameless impersonation of having laboured long and hard in Piers' campaign.

In reality, the person Amanda Dundas had been campaigning for was herself, Suzy thought caustically. Determined to become a top actress, though so far stardom had steadfastly refused to beckon, she had capitalised on Piers' situation by raking in all possible publicity—with the aim of boosting her career. However, while her motives had been recognised, and condemned, by those in the know, no one was going to reveal such a cruel truth to a returned hostage. This meant Piers would remain unaware, and be highly appreciative of his girlfriend's phoney and yet much flaunted support.

'What would you have thought?' Piers prompted.

'Er—that if you're going to be in London for the next month, you must be able to spare the occasional morning or afternoon,' Suzy quickly adjusted.

'I could,' he agreed, and paused. 'However, I'm not going to.'

'You've spoken to just about everyone else, so why shut the door on me?' she protested.

'I spoke to them on the understanding that once I left the clinic, I'd be left alone.'

'But——'

'I thought you said that if I was sick and tired of talking, you'd understand? Guess what, I am sick and tired—of this conversation.' Piers looked at the watch which was strapped to his broad, hair-sprinkled wrist. 'Isn't it time you were on your way to Fulham, Sparky?'

Suzy's hands crunched into irritated fists. Three years ago, Piers had called her 'Sparky'. Then she had regarded the word as an endearment and had actually, pathetically, liked it, but now it could be recognised as a tag bestowed by a patronising male. How dared he patronise her, she thought furiously, and how dared he refuse to be in her book? A couple of hours ago she might have been fighting against his inclusion, but now she had reconsidered and, perhaps spurred in part by his rebuffs, had executed an about-turn. Randolph had been right, a profile on Piers Armstrong would add an extra dimension and some pizzazz. It would improve the book, and her writer's blood was up. He *must* be included. And if she happened to make some money out of him along the way—well, it would be poetic justice!

'Suppose I show you my manuscript?' she suggested, certain that, no matter what he had said, his opinion of her writing capabilities must be the real stumbling block. 'Then you'll know I'm not in the

business of sensationalising or sentimentalising.' She
shone a smile of what was intended to be melting
sweetness. 'How'd it be if I drop a copy in to you
tomorrow?'

Piers walked across the room towards her. 'You're
hellbent on coaxing me to be profiled?' he said.

Suzy hesitated, aware of a nuance and yet unable
to understand. 'You could say that,' she agreed
guardedly.

He dropped down opposite her on the sofa, his
hands languorously parked in his jeans pockets and
his long legs stretched out. 'The way you were hellbent
on coaxing me once before?' he enquired, in a soft,
menacing tone. 'The way you seduced me into doing
something which I had strong doubts about, but which
you very much desired?'

Memories ricocheted through her mind and a hot
wave of colour flooded up her throat. Now she
understood exactly what he was talking about. How
could she ever have been so shameless, so wanton?
she wondered . . . and so heartbreakingly innocent.

'Not like that,' she said, checking her watch again,
which meant she did not need to look at him.

'In order to achieve your objective, you won't be
wearing a knock-'em-dead dress?' taunted Piers, the
menace in his voice hardening into cold con-
temptuous steel. 'Or stroking your fingers along my
thigh, or——'

Suzy's head jerked up and she met his gaze. She
would not be intimidated or flustered or deterred by
this reference to the past.

'You've made an extremely lucrative living out of
people talking to you,' she said, attempting to per-

suade him and yet sound nonchalant at one and the
same time, which was rather like tightrope-walking
on a rubber band, 'so don't you think it's only fair
that I should be given the chance to——'

A snarl unleashed itself from the back of his throat
and he sat up straight. 'You talk about fairness? You
want to use me,' he stated, 'the way you used me once
before.'

Reaction against his charge kicked against her
stomach, yet Suzy refused to respond. There was
nothing to be gained from opening old wounds. But
Piers Armstrong had not forgotten her. On the contrary, he appeared to possess total recall of what had
happened between them three years ago, and it
rankled. Infuriated. Had festered. She cast him a look.
This seemed strange, for, whatever the depth of her
hurt, the only damage he had suffered was a small
knock to his ego which, at the time, he had taken in
his stride.

'All the other men in my book have said that talking
to me was therapy,' she persisted.

'Bully for them—however, I'm not in need of
therapy,' he replied. 'And if I were, the last person
I'd choose as my shrink is you.'

'But——'

'Am I talking in code?' Piers demanded. 'I'm not
giving you your interviews. This time—*this time*,' he
said, repeating the words with blistering emphasis,
'you're going to have to manage without me.'

Suzy gathered up her bag, swept to her feet and,
with her head held high, marched to the door. 'And
I will!' she declared.

CHAPTER TWO

THE machine swallowed her ticket, and Suzy walked through the barrier, up the stairs and out of the Underground station into the summer sunshine. Hooking the strap of her beige leather satchel more securely on to her shoulder, she set off towards Regent's Park and the grand Nash terrace where Hugo Armstrong had his home.

Last week, in the split-second after the returned hostage had so forcibly told her that she must manage without him, Suzy had realised that she could—and still include him in her book. As there were plenty of unauthorised biographies around, so she could write an unauthorised profile—*if* she read up on what had already been published about him, and *if* his family and friends were prepared to talk.

When Randolph Gardener had rung the next morning to ask how she had got on at the clinic, Suzy had floated her plan.

'It's not the ideal,' she admitted, 'but I see no reason why Piers' lack of co-operation should be allowed to kill the project stone dead.'

'Neither do I,' the editorial director agreed, and had proceeded to voice his full support.

On jettisoning the telephone, Suzy had swung into action. Her time as a reporter had left her with plenty of contacts among the fraternity, so she had embarked on a journey which had taken her from one newspaper office to the next; though, wary of entering Piers' territory, she had avoided *The View*. People were consulted and articles photocopied until, two days later, she had assembled a comprehensive file which detailed the circumstances of Piers' kidnap and release, his responses at the airport press conference, and just about every other of his utterances which had since appeared in print. She had spent the weekend poring over the file and making notes, and on Monday morning had moved on to that second and vital 'if'—talking to his family and associates.

The first and obvious person for her to approach was Hugo Armstrong, with whom, when interviewing him a year ago, she had established an immediate rapport. Why this should have happened she did not know, Suzy thought as she walked along, for, on the face of it, he was not at all her kind of person. A stereotypical *ac-tor* of the old school, everything about Hugo was larger than life. His gestures were dramatic, his choice of words flamboyant, he seemed to be forever striding around on his own invisible piece of stage. Yet she had warmed to him—and he to her—and, when his son had disappeared, she had gone round the very next day to offer her sympathy. After thanking her, Hugo had spoken of his wish to mount a campaign, and Suzy had found herself saying she would like to help; so they had met intermittently ever since.

A line cut between her brows. At the time, Hugo had also told her that instead of him being close to his only child, which was what he had previously and publicly asserted, their relationship was strained. With tears glistening in his eyes, he had confessed that they rarely met, and whenever they did Piers was aloof. The trouble lay in the past. Apparently, after only a few years of marriage Hugo had, without warning and giving no reason, abandoned his wife Diana, who, less than two years later, had been tragically killed in a car accident—at which time he had despatched his young son to boarding school. On reaching manhood, Piers had accused his father of showing a selfish disregard both as a husband and a parent; and thereafter kept his distance. It was a distance which the older man longed to narrow and had attempted to narrow, but Piers remained unresponsive. Had the events of the past year brought about a reconciliation? Suzy wondered hopefully. After the traumas both father and son had gone through, it seemed possible.

Reaching the park, Suzy followed a path which circumnavigated the pond. Although yesterday Hugo Armstrong had responded to her request for a next-day interview with an affable affirmative, since then she had been on tenterhooks. Honesty had insisted she alert him to his son's opposition, so might he reconsider and change his mind? Or, more to the point, if—when—he mentioned her call, would Piers change his mind for him? Even before setting off this morning, she had wondered whether the phone might ring and the interview would be regretfully cancelled, but her fears had proved groundless. She crossed her fingers. So far, so good.

When she had originally met the actor and given him her name she had, she recalled, wondered if he might recognise it. He had not. Though why should he? Suzy thought drily, as she headed across the daisy-dotted grass towards the park's eastern perimeter.

Piers' history was littered with girlfriends and, two years earlier, he would not have bothered to mention the guileless young blonde who had been just one more. Her ivory silk shirt was tucked tighter into the waistband of her short beige skirt. She had seen no point in telling his father of the long-defunct connection, and later the moment for revelation had passed. Hugo was aware that she and Piers had once worked on the same newspaper, but that was all.

The terrace of pristine white town houses overlooked the green pastures of the park, and Suzy made her way along to one where well-manicured box trees guarded the porch. Mounting the stone steps, she pressed her finger on a gleaming brass bell. A minute or so later, footsteps sounded and the front door swung open to reveal Hugo Armstrong, immaculate in a navy blazer, pearl-grey flannels and with a blue and grey silk cravat knotted around his neck. While their styles of dress were very different, he could be immediately identified as Piers' father. It was not so much his facial features—only their noses were similar—but his long-limbed ease and size. Both were well-built and carried themselves with the aplomb of tall men.

'You're wonderfully punctual,' Hugo boomed, in the treacle-rich voice which was famed for its ability to reach the rear stalls.

'Thank you for seeing me at such short notice,' Suzy said, as he kissed her on both cheeks and welcomed her inside.

'It's always a delight to see you, my dear,' he replied, the twinkle in his eyes making it plain that he retained an ongoing appreciation of the fairer sex, despite being in his sixties and despite having a mistress.

In his love-'em-and-leave-'em attitude Piers was following in his father's footsteps, for ever since his wife's death Hugo had gone from one amorous alliance to another. Each was recorded in the gossip columns with salacious glee. Each had eventually come a cropper. However, for over three years now, which constituted a record, he had been sharing his home with Barbara Dane, a fifty-something choreographer.

'It's fortunate you didn't ask for a chat a week ago,' Hugo continued. 'I'm rehearsing a new play, and at the time we were having the most tremendous problems with the second lead. To say the chap's acting was wooden would be an insult to trees, and—— '

Humorously describing the angst which he and everyone else in the cast had suffered before the culprit had finally got to grips with his part, he ushered her along a chandeliered hall and through an archway into an opulently decorated green and gold drawing-room.

'Babs is out, she's due back soon, and on her return she'll make us a flagon of coffee,' said Hugo, tugging at the razor-sharp creases of his trousers as he sat down opposite Suzy in a gold brocade armchair. 'She's gone to pore over menus with the caterers. You see, although Piers doesn't know it, we're planning a mammoth welcome-home shindig.'

Suzy smiled. A party seemed to indicate that the rift with his son had finally been healed—thank goodness! She was tempted to tell Hugo how happy she felt for him, but hesitated. While at the time of

Piers' disappearance he had spoken about the discord frankly and at length, he had never mentioned it again. Indeed, his staunch avoidance of the subject had made her realise that his confessions must have spilled out in a weak moment and were regretted. Confessing to flaws was not his style.

'Sounds like fun,' she remarked.

'It'll be a truly memorable occasion,' Hugo enthused, and leant forward. 'You won't say anything about it to anyone?'

'Not a word,' Suzy assured him.

'Thank you, my dear, and in return I promise not to tell my son and heir about this little tête-à-tête.'

As she took her notebook and tape recorder from her bag, Suzy grinned. 'Thank *you*.'

Although it seemed inevitable that the subject of her profile would find out what she was doing sooner or later—someone was bound to give the game away— if his father kept quiet then she might be able to log several more interviews without his knowledge. And the more she managed to log while Piers remained unaware, the better.

'Shoot,' the actor instructed, settling comfortably back in his armchair, as he must have settled back to give a thousand and one other interviews over the years.

'How did you feel when you first heard that Piers had been snatched?' asked Suzy, as her machine began to whirr.

When she had called round it had been obvious how Hugo had felt—shaky, beside himself with anxiety, completely thrown—but, of course, he had to describe his reaction in his own words.

'Shocked—what father wouldn't be?—but not too perturbed. Piers is entirely capable of taking care of himself. Wry in calamity, nonchalant in triumph, and always in control,' Hugo enunciated, sounding as though he might be quoting lines from a play in which he had appeared.

Suzy blinked. Although the description of his son struck her as apt, this was not the kind of answer she had expected.

'The thought of him being held hostage didn't keep you awake at night?' she protested.

'Indeed, no. I never had any doubts but that he'd survive unharmed, and I always knew he'd come through it beautifully, which he has.'

Her brow furrowed. Clearly Hugo had stepped on to his own private piece of stage and was playing the supportive parent of the noble son to the hilt. It might be an amazingly persuasive performance, but if her profile were to have any credibility it was vital he be honest.

'My parents would have been pacing the floor, unable to concentrate, jellies of neuroses for the entire year,' Suzy said, attempting to coax him into an admission of equivalent distress.

'Maybe, but——' The blazered shoulders moved in an elegant shrug.

She changed tack. 'Could you tell me what Piers was like as a child?'

'Never caused any trouble. Unfortunately my career meant I was unable to give him as much time as I would have liked, so after Diana died he virtually brought himself up, and made a bloody fine job of it,' Hugo declared.

'How old was Piers when his mother died?' Suzy enquired, realising that she did not know.

Though how much did she know about him? she thought. Not a great deal. Three years ago, the demands of Piers' career had meant that the number of hours they had actually spent together had been few. Then they had been busy catching up on what each of them had been doing and there had never been much opportunity to swap background information.

'He was eight. A mature eight.' Hugo adjusted the line of a snowy white cuff. 'He excelled at school.'

'In which way?' she queried.

'In every way. Piers not only shone in his studies, but at sports—all sports.'

Suzy asked another question and another, but to her rising desperation and with her heart sinking, the interview continued with Hugo lavishing fulsome praise. Whether in his youth, as a journalist, or doing his period as a hostage, his son had been out-and-out perfection. She knew otherwise, she thought acidly, but no matter how hard she tried there was no way the actor could be induced to contribute anything which was not exaggerated and which sounded *real*—about Piers, about anything. And, of course, the friction which had existed between them was wholly ignored.

'Each profile is being illustrated with a page of photographs, so do you have any snaps which I could use?' she requested, when she had reached the end of her questions and, ruefully acknowledging defeat, had switched off her machine. 'Both when Piers was young and up to the present day.'

'There are some in my study,' said Hugo, with a
smile. He was rising to his feet, when the door bell
suddenly pealed. 'This'll be Babs,' he said, diverted.
'She's always forgetting her key. Please excuse me.'

He disappeared, but a moment or two later the surprised rumble of his baritone down the hall indicated
that whoever it was who had arrived, it could not be
his present partner. Suzy put her notebook away in
her bag. Her job was done, the actor had a visitor,
and she was intruding. As soon as the photographs
had been provided, she would leave.

'Guess who's here,' boomed Hugo, striding back
in to flourish a delighted arm. 'Haven't seen him since
he was discharged from the clinic, so he's more than
welcome.'

As a tall lean-hipped man in a black polo-shirt and
blue jeans strolled in through the archway, Suzy's
stomach hollowed. Her head pounded. She gave a
silent protesting wail. Another five minutes and she
would have been gone, so why must Piers choose this
particular time on this particular morning to pay his
father a visit? Why must he catch her red-handed?
Why, when Hugo had so obligingly offered to remain
silent, did he have to be alerted to her strategy so *soon*?

The new arrival stopped dead. He frowned at her,
down at the tape recorder, then angry grey eyes swept
back up to nail themselves to hers.

'There's no need to ask what you're doing,' he said,
in a damning indictment.

Suzy sat straighter. His displeasure did not mean
she had to feel ashamed, or guilty—nor that she
must apologise.

'I'm only doing it because you've given me no alternative,' she retorted, forcing herself to gaze steadily back.

Piers swung to his father. 'You won't know this, but Miss Collier——' his enunciation of her surname was harsh and distancing '—has already asked me if I'd agree to be interviewed for her book, and I flatly refused.'

'You're wrong, old boy, I do know,' Hugo told him, with an awkward smile.

'I explained that you weren't in favour when I telephoned to fix the interview,' said Suzy.

Piers scowled at her, then turned back to his father. 'Yet you were still willing to speak?' he demanded.

'You may insist on hiding your light under a bushel, but I see no earthly reason why I shouldn't say a few words about my brave son,' Hugo protested, his pride shining through. 'Isn't it time you paid a visit to the barber?' he continued. 'I don't deny that your hair looks dashing in a cavalier sort of way, but——'

'Never mind my hair,' Piers cut in. 'What we're talking about is your agreeing to assist with a profile which I have not sanctioned and which I do not want!'

'But this is your fifteen minutes of fame which Andy Warhol promised everyone back in the Sixties, and one profile in one book isn't going to cause you any bother,' said his father, obviously reluctant to quarrel. 'Besides, Suzy's a friend of mine, and she helped in your campaign, and——'

'I just typed a few letters,' Suzy said, in quick dismissal. She had no intention of trading on what she had done—which she would have done for anyone. 'All the profile means is that you may be mentioned in a review some time next year,' she went on. 'If my book's lucky enough to be reviewed.'

'It will be,' Hugo assured her gallantly. 'You asked for photographs,' he said, remembering. 'I'll go and get them.'

'You may not have won any prizes, but you're a dead cert for the Sneak of the Year Award!' rasped Piers the moment they were alone.

'Just because you didn't bestow your blessing on the profile, you expected me to abandon it?' Suzy protested.

'Damn right! Coming to see my father behind my back is——'

'Although I may have failed to despatch a fax giving you advance notice of our meeting today, he could have told you,' she defended. 'I didn't ask him to keep quiet, as I shan't be asking anyone else I interview to keep quiet either.'

'You intend to cast your net wider and drag in other people?' Piers demanded.

Her chin lifted. 'I'm sorry if it offends your sensibilities, but yes.'

A muscle clenched in his jaw and his grey eyes darkened to leaden black. If he had been a pirate, there was no doubt her insubordination would have been punished by her being keelhauled or made to walk the plank.

'I've heard all about the fearless spirit of investigation,' he bit out, 'but——'

'Let me ask you something,' said Suzy, rising to her feet because sitting below him while he stood was making her feel disadvantaged—and disadvantages were the last thing she needed right now. 'If you required comments and you were unable to obtain them from the source, wouldn't you go elsewhere? Of course you would. And the fact that you knew the source would be . . . rattled wouldn't stop you.'

'In other words, all's fair in love, war and writing profiles?' Piers said tersely.

'In other words, I don't need your seal of approval,' she told him.

'You're not going to get it!' He strode forward to plant himself in front of her, six foot three inches of aggressive, angry, dominant male. 'Erase everything you have on that tape,' he ordered.

Although it required an effort, Suzy stood firm. Piers Armstrong had a reputation for never allowing himself to be pushed around, and she did not intend to be pushed around either. Three years ago, she would have given way and obeyed his command, but these days she was made of sterner stuff.

'You're acting the heavy?' she enquired.

'You're the one who wants to play rough, lady, not me,' he responded. 'Now, wipe that damn tape.'

Her eyes met his in a look of cool determination. 'No,' she said.

Piers bent to the machine, pushed a button and the cover flipped open. 'In that case, I'll take it.'

'You can't!' wailed Suzy.

'Watch me,' he said, and slid the tape into his hip pocket.

Her temper flared. There was nothing of Hugo's spiel which she intended to quote verbatim, so the tape had little real value, but that was not the point. The point was that Piers was interfering with the gathering of her data, with the writing of her book.

'Would you kindly return *my* property?' she demanded heatedly. He shook his head. 'In that case, I'll take it,' Suzy declared, spitting his own words back to him, and made a sudden lunge for his pocket.

Taken by surprise, Piers reared back, started to turn and stumbled. Overbalancing, he made an instinctive grab at her in an attempt to remain upright, but only succeeded in yanking her off balance too.

'Aargh!' she gasped, as he toppled back on to the sofa and she fell on top of him.

Winded, she lay there for a moment or two, then she half raised herself.

'No, you don't,' said Piers, when her hand dived downwards in a lightning attack on his hip pocket.

He caught hold of her wrists and pinioned her arms behind her back. Furiously wriggling and squirming, Suzy struggled to wrench an arm free and, thanks to a sly kick at his shins which made him swear and momentarily distracted him, she managed it.

'I do!' she retorted, going in search of the tape again.

Piers recaptured her arm with indolent ease. 'I love to feel the heat of a woman's anger,' he remarked.

As his hands curved tightly around the slender bones of her wrists, Suzy's eyes shot daggers. She had never met anyone more condescending, more arrogant, or more infuriating!

'I understood that seduction was no longer your stock-in-trade,' remarked Piers, as she once more started to squirm.

'It—it isn't,' she panted.

'So you aren't slithering around in order to arouse me?' he asked.

Suzy tugged and twisted her arms, but to no avail. He had twice her physical strength. 'Of course not.'

'But we are two different genders, and it's red blood which flows in my veins,' he murmured.

Her fighting ceased and she lay still—very still. Somewhat belatedly, his remark had alerted her to the fact that Piers *was* aroused. Suzy's heart thumped wildly in her chest. Why, when at the clinic she had shied away from so much as shaking his hand, had she launched such a physical protest? she wondered. Why, instead of leaping straight up when they fell down, had she continued to lie on top of him, continued to grab for his hip pocket?

'I'm simply attempting to retrieve my tape,' she told him, with as much dignity as she could muster. Though, with her hair falling into her eyes and her cheeks bright red, it was a preciously small amount.

'And how do you explain acting the *femme fatale*?'

Suzy looked up into the pale grey eyes which were just a few inches from hers. '*Femme fatale*? I don't know what you mean.'

Piers removed one of the restraining hands from her wrists and brought it between them. 'I mean this,' he said, running the tip of a long index finger slowly down her throat and into the warm valley between her breasts.

She jerked back. His touch—so casual and yet so intimate—was like an electric shock. She felt as if he had sent a live current zig-zagging through every cell of her body. As his finger had stroked down so had his eyes, and now, as she followed his gaze, her face flamed. The top three buttons at the neck of her shirt were open, revealing the creamy swell of her breasts in what suddenly seemed like a racily low-cut white lace bra.

'I wasn't aware the buttons were undone,' she said stiffly.

'They came undone when you made that first grab. The glimpse of bosom has been most alluring, though the only time you lapsed into full-blown eroticism was when you pushed yourself up and then——' Piers rolled his eyes.

'You can have the tape,' Suzy told him, at speed. 'And you can release me.'

'But after so much celibacy, to have a curvy young woman spreadeagled on top of me is most... invigorating,' he drawled, and shifted his body against hers.

As she felt the thrust of him, a wave of heat engulfed her.

'Let me go!' she demanded, in a mixture of panic and fury.

A lazy smile tilted the corners of his mouth. 'You aren't inclined to indulge me?'

'No, I am not!'

'Spoilsport,' said Piers, and released her.

Back on her feet, Suzy hastily fastened the buttons and tucked her shirt back into her skirt. Today her hair was worn loose, and she attempted to smooth down the tousled wheat-gold strands.

'Aren't you being a touch paranoid about my profile?' she demanded, when her composure had been reassembled—well, some of it.

Piers rose from the sofa. 'Paranoid?' he repeated, his eyes glittering dangerously.

'Suzy's right,' said Hugo, breezing back into the room with a handful of photographs. 'You're taking this business of being written up far too seriously. Even if you did possess some murky secret——' he chuckled '—I've had enough experience of being interviewed to know when to be discreet.'

Piers frowned. 'Yes, you're good at discretion,' he remarked. 'For example, you've said nothing to me about the welcome-home party which you and Barbara are so busily arranging.'

His father's jaw dropped. 'You know about that?'

'It's the reason I'm here,' said Piers. 'While I've no wish to appear ungracious, I've come to suggest you cancel it, because I shan't be present on the night.'

'But Babs and I thought you'd enjoy hobnobbing with some of your chums again,' Hugo protested, sounding so disappointed that Suzy's heart shrivelled.

She eyed the two men. Granted, her presence had annoyed Piers, but, that apart, his manner towards his father was a little removed and very proper. And Hugo appeared...wary. He had said they had not met since Piers had left the clinic. Maybe it was only a couple of days, but in the circumstances... Suzy sighed. It seemed that the burying of differences which Hugo longed for, and which she had hoped for, had not come to pass.

All of a sudden, Piers noticed her inspection. He shot her a probing glance, then took a step towards his father.

'Dad, I'm sorry,' he said, his tone gentler and more apologetic, 'but right now the prospect of spending an evening in a room full of people doesn't turn me on.'

Hugo looked bewildered. 'Why ever not?'

'Because after being isolated for so long with just one person, I think I'd find it claustrophobic. And I wouldn't want to put a dampener on everything by breaking out in a cold sweat and having to make a hurried exit midway.'

His father smiled. 'I understand,' he said.

Suzy frowned. If any other ex-hostage had made such a claim she would have believed them, but was Piers telling the truth? And if not, had he said what he did because he had felt ill at ease with Hugo's dismay and needed to comfort him, or was it more a matter of making an excuse for her benefit? While she had told him about her family in what now seemed embarrassing detail, throughout their three-month affair Piers had rarely mentioned his father; yet when he did there had been no hint of bad feeling. He too obviously preferred to keep it hidden.

'You must tell me who snitched,' Hugo said bluffly, then stopped at the sound of the front door being opened. 'Babs is back,' he declared.

A few moments later, a trim, compact-bodied woman came into the room. Her ash-blonde hair made a froth of short curls around her head and she wore a pale green button-through dress.

'Hello, angel,' said Hugo, affectionately catching hold of her hand.

'Hello, my pet. Sorry I took so long.' She kissed him, then reached up to deposit a kiss on Piers' cheek. 'I didn't expect to find you here,' she said, darting a smile back at his father, 'but what a lovely surprise!' She grinned at Suzy. 'It's good to see you again.'

'And you,' Suzy said sincerely, for, although she did not know her well, she had found Barbara to be unassuming and friendly.

'I'm afraid your conference with the caterers has been wasted,' said Hugo. 'You see, Piers has heard about the party and wants to be excused. Doesn't feel up to socialising just yet.'

'Oh, no!' Barbara exclaimed.

'It's understandable,' he said loyally.

Piers raised his eyebrows. 'Forgive me?'

Barbara laughed. 'I'd forgive you anything when you look at me in that appealing little-boy way.' She turned towards the kitchen. 'You must all be gasping for a coffee.'

'Not for me, thanks,' Suzy said quickly. 'I have work to do and I ought to get home. If I could have the photographs,' she added, reminding Hugo that he was still holding them.

'I hope you find something suitable,' he said, as he passed them over. 'If not, give me a ring and——' he winked '—I'll see what other snaps I can find of Superman.'

'Dad——' Piers began.

Suzy hastily stashed the photos and her tape recorder into her bag. 'It was kind of you to spare me so much time,' she said to her host, and flashed a general smile. 'Goodbye.'

As she ran down the steps, she made a face. She did not want to spend the next two months under siege, but the battle lines had been drawn and now it seemed that Piers would go all out to do whatever he could to thwart her, to harass, to make compiling the case history as difficult as possible. He was involved in what was called 'getting even', and just because his masculine pride had once been slighted! She strode along the street. When held hostage he would have had more than enough time to track back over the episode with her, yet he had never seemed like a man to be upset by inconsequentials. Her stomach nipped. And she *had* been inconsequential, she had proof of that.

All of a sudden a large hand landed on her shoulder, stopping her in her tracks.

'I'll run you home,' said Piers.

Startled, Suzy turned to shine a wavering smile. 'Thanks for the offer, but I know your father would like your company, and I can easily take the Underground, and it's a lovely day for a walk,' she gabbled.

He had brought her to a halt beside a dark green sports car which she recognised as familiar, and he bent to unlock the passenger door.

'Get in,' he instructed, in a voice which warned that if she did not comply she could find herself being unceremoniously bundled inside.

Her skirt was short and tight, and the car was low. How could she get in gracefully? Suzy wondered. It was impossible. Aware of him waiting and revealing far more leg than she would have wished in his presence, she did as she was told.

'Since when have you been such a scheming, ring-a-ding-ding, bloody-minded go-getter?' demanded Piers, climbing in beside her. 'The Suzy I used to know would never——'

'The Suzy you used to know is a big girl now,' she told him.

His eyes dropped to the jut of her breasts beneath the silk shirt. 'Not that much bigger,' he remarked. 'Still around thirty-six rosy-tipped inches, if I'm not mistaken?'

Suzy's face burned. She had not wanted to accept the lift, and now she was trapped. Trapped in the sports car's intimate interior with a man who was much too close for comfort, much too disturbing, far too provocative. Ten years her senior and more experienced in every way, Piers Armstrong had an inherently urbane attitude towards matters physical and sexual. Back in time, he had enjoyed shocking her and making her blush, and it was maddening to know that he still possessed the knack. But the image she wanted to project was that of a poised, self-contained woman, not a pink-cheeked, flustered girl!

'I'm sorry if I've invoked your wrath,' she said, hurriedly steering the conversation elsewhere. Anywhere else. 'But I do have a remit for the profile from my publishers.'

Piers twisted the key in the ignition, and the car roared to life. 'Tell them it's no go.'

'I can't.'

'You mean you won't,' he said, turning the wheel with strong hands and drawing away from the kerb.

Suzy shot a defiant look at his profile. 'While I may have to go into hiding and avoid standing in front of lighted windows, short of homicide there's nothing you can do to stop me writing about you. Nor does it matter that you've confiscated my tape,' she went on, 'because I have a record of everything your father said stored in here——' she tapped her head '—and he said some very interesting things.'

'I can imagine,' Piers remarked tersely.

'How you progressed from being a model schoolboy to dicing with death as a fearless war correspondent,' Suzy recited, and her mouth suddenly dimpled. 'Bullets part your hair, but do you worry? You do not. And as for being held hostage—it was child's play. Which should all make for a most exhilarating account.'

'I don't want to be portrayed as some kind of a hero,' he rasped.

She opened wide blue eyes. 'Whatever gave you that idea?'

'Hugo's a past master at putting his own interpretation on things,' Piers said impatiently, 'but I can assure you that whatever he's said, it'll be more fiction than fact.'

'And you're afraid my profile will be awash with adulation?' Suzy's mouth dimpled again. 'I have to admit that your father did provide some wonderfully choice phrases about the son whom he appears to regard as little short of a deity.' Her smile faded as she remembered that the adulation was not returned. 'Why aren't you going to his party?' she questioned.

Piers frowned ahead through the windscreen. 'You heard what I said—because I could feel hemmed in.'

'But——'

'And although Hugo reckoned the occasion was in order for me to meet up with my friends, it's more likely to be an excuse for him to invite round his buddies,' he added.

'Even so, he'd be delighted if you went, even for an hour, and he has worked so hard on your behalf— *genuinely* worked,' Suzy stressed, then frowned aware

that by implying that others had falsified their en-
deavours—namely, Amanda Dundas—she could
provoke awkward questions. 'I know that your release, like your kidnap, was at random and can't be
attributed to the campaign,' she carried on, 'but it
doesn't invalidate your father's efforts.'

Piers' grip tightened markedly around the steering
wheel. 'I'm grateful for everything he did,' he said,
'very grateful, and I've told him. Are you thinking
of putting some personal reminiscences into your
profile?'

'Sorry?' It took a moment for her to make the
necessary mental leap. 'Oh, no, it's not a kiss-and-
tell.'

He shot her a dry look. 'How about a kick-and-
tell?'

'That neither. I'm well aware that people's lives are
not mine to dissect and spread out for the public to
see,' said Suzy, her tone serious. 'So you need have
no fears, because I shan't be overly intrusive.'

'You expect me to fall at your feet and blubber my
thanks?' Piers enquired.

'I expect you to remember that what you're cre-
ating such a fuss about is a profile which will be one
of six,' she responded. 'It's not as though I'm making
you the subject of an entire book.' A smile teased the
edges of her mouth. 'Though maybe I should.'

'And what happens after that? You sell the screen
rights and Hollywood makes a movie?' he said drolly.

She grinned. 'I'd settle for a TV mini-series.'

As they swept down past the luxury hotels of Park
Lane and on to the huge roundabout of Hyde Park
Corner, Suzy edged an inch or two closer to the door.

Every time her escort changed gear, he brushed against her. She felt a tremor of resentment at his size. Why did he have to be so big, so overwhelmingly male, so in control? Her eyes went to the tanned fingers which moved the gear-stick and controlled the wheel. Those were the fingers which had once controlled *her*, she thought, which had once lifted her up into realms of ecstasy she had never known existed.

'You seem to have dropped straight back into driving,' she remarked, needing to talk in order to obliterate the images which had begun to dance through her mind.

Piers nodded. 'Surprisingly I feel perfectly at ease,' he said, as he threaded the sports car adroitly through the interweaving lanes of cars, buses and black taxi-cabs, 'even in this crush.'

And I bet you'd also feel at ease in a group of people, Suzy thought, now even more suspicious of his 'hemmed-in' claim.

'It's reckoned to take one month to adjust to each year spent away,' she observed, and cast him a look. 'Would you agree? Would you say that although you've spent the month in a clinic, you've made the adjustment and are able to cope with the demands of everyday life again? Or is there something which worries you?'

'Pass,' he said.

'Pardon me?'

'You think I'm going to be tricked into providing data to be used in your profile?' Piers shook his head. 'From now on, I'm telling you zilch.'

'But I was only——'

'*Zilch.*'

'So if I didn't already know how old you were, you wouldn't tell me?' Suzy protested.

'Nope. The only way you'd find out is if you cut me in half and counted the rings.'

She sighed. She had asked out of general interest, that was all, but if he chose to consider her devious, so be it.

A silence formed, and they motored on; heading south and crossing one of the bridges which spanned the wide blue ribbon of the Thames.

'How are you progressing with your flat-hunting?' asked Piers, as they reached Putney's narrow bustling High Street.

She grimaced. 'Both the Fulham ones were shoeboxes, and the half-dozen I've seen since haven't been much bigger. There must be an affordable flat with enough room for my modest collection of worldly goods somewhere in London, but I've yet to find it.' She pointed ahead up the hill. ''You take the second turn on the right, after the traffic lights.'

He nodded. 'I remember.'

She had memories too, Suzy thought, as he negotiated the corner. Of how, on another occasion, she had sat beside Piers in the sports car. Of how, on another occasion, he had driven her to her flat. Of how she had so determinedly kissed him and coaxed him and——

'Who are you planning to speak to next,' he enquired, swinging into the kerb and cutting the engine, 'Amanda?'

Her stomach cramped. It had been obvious from the start that the actress would need to be approached, yet she had shied away from thinking about it. Suzy unclipped her seatbelt. Amanda Dundas might not remember, but she had interviewed her once before. *The View*'s women's page had done a feature on the lifestyles of female celebrities, and she had been sent to ask her about the kind of clothes she wore, what she kept on her dressing-table, her favourite cosmetics and such. The answers she received were unremarkable; it was what the brunette had said conspiratorially and in passing which had brought her world crashing down. Suzy winced. Even now, three years later, the memory of what she had learned sliced into her like a knife.

'I haven't fixed any more interviews yet,' she answered, stalling.

'I don't want you to speak to her,' said Piers.

His jaw had taken on a granite edge and determination oozed from every pore. It had been noticeable in the newspaper cuttings she had read how he had parried any questions concerning him and his girlfriend, and that there had been a dearth of quotes. Presumably he had asked the reporters to keep his private life private. She could understand him not wanting it to become common property, but——

'That's an order?' Suzy pressed down on the handle and opened the door. 'Sorry, I won't be bullied.'

'It isn't an order.' Piers hesitated. 'It's a request.'

She had been about to clamber from the vehicle, but now she stopped. He was *asking* her to steer clear, although it had taken an effort—but why? All he had to do was tell his girlfriend he would prefer her not to see her and Amanda would agree. Or would she? Suzy frowned. The actress appeared to regard any media coverage as fertile hunting ground in her pursuit of fame, and although a mention in a book lacked the impact of a TV appearance, she could be tempted. Suzy sighed. Apart from her instinctive aversion to confronting Amanda again, even if a meeting could be arranged, doubtless all she would hear would be the same kind of useless inflated sentences which Hugo had spouted.

'I won't speak to her,' she agreed.

'Thank you,' Piers said gravely. 'My father may have provided a photograph of me dressed as an elf——'

'Kinky!'

'—at the age of three,' he completed. 'I'd be grateful if you could give that a miss too.'

When Barbara had spoken of his 'little boy' appeal, she had been referring to the way Piers had of slanting up his eyebrows and giving a crooked smile which made him look vulnerable. It was a look which, in his role as a journalist, had resulted in people telling him far more than they would have done otherwise. Suzy knew it could be described as a brilliantly effective technique, but it was the way he was looking at her now, and, to her annoyance, she found it well nigh irresistible.

'Done, but those are the only concessions,' she declared, determined not to be swayed again. 'I've put a lot of hard work and tender loving care into my book, and no matter how many obstacles you may attempt to place in my way, I shall be including a section on you.'

The 'little boy' look vanished. 'So it's role model—Lucretia Borgia? Motto—what I want I'll get?' Piers taunted, as she climbed from the car. He thrust the gearstick into first. 'Fine, I know where I stand,' he said, and, with a squeal of tyres, he sped away.

CHAPTER THREE

HER elbows on the desk and her chin resting on her hands, Suzy frowned at the sheet of paper that sat in her typewriter. What else had Hugo Armstrong said? It was mid-afternoon and she was attempting to recall their conversation earlier in the day. It did not matter that the resultant transcript was destined to be filed away and never used; her professionalism demanded that a record be made. But how did she incorporate Hugo in her profile? Suzy brooded. Some reference needed to be made, for as he was Piers' closest relative it would seem odd if he was ignored. A sigh escaped. If only she could describe how devastated he had been by his son's kidnap, but to do so when he had given her such a robustly upbeat account would be unethical. Should she go and see him again and explain her need for warts-and-all realism? she wondered. But would he admit to warts? It seemed doubtful.

Suzy's gaze swung to the list of people whom she had identified as desirable interviewees. Instead of fretting about Hugo, she ought to be ringing them—and hope that she was one jump ahead of his son. Her hand was outstretched in readiness when the phone suddenly rang.

'It's Piers,' a voice said, when she lifted the receiver.

Suzy tensed, she could not help herself. 'What do you want?' she asked.

'Could you come to my apartment tomorrow afternoon at, say, around three?'

'Er. . . yes.' Her brow furrowed. 'But what for?'

'I'll explain then,' said Piers, and the line went dead.

Heavy bronze doors slid silently closed and the lift began its ascent. Suzy chewed at her lip in a fretful gesture. After a night spent tossing and turning and endless consideration, she still felt unsure about the wisdom of responding to Piers' summons. Biographers of reluctant subjects were known to receive pre-publication legal letters, so when she arrived at the fifth-floor apartment in a few seconds' time would she find herself faced by a lawyer and handed a stern warning which threatened all kinds of reprisals? In writing about the war correspondent she was not breaking the law and nothing in her account would be libellous, so any warning would merely be sabre-rattling. Even so, the profile had already caused her enough nervous strain, and she did not want to feel even more hounded. Or manacled. Or restricted. Her thoughts skittered sideways. Neither was she keen to meet Amanda Dundas again.

Raising her eyes, Suzy watched the illuminated floor numbers change. Two, three, four. In addition, coming to here this afternoon was inconvenient. The likelihood of her finding a new flat and relocating within the next week was now nil and, although it had slipped her mind when Piers had phoned, she had arranged for a representative from a removal company to call round at three o'clock to give her a quotation for putting her goods in store. The man could only come in the afternoons, so she had been forced to rearrange the appointment for tomorrow.

The lift slowed to a halt, and she stepped out into the small private entrance lobby. Her hair was lifted from the collar of her khaki jumpsuit. Her backbone was straightened. No matter what confronted her, she refused to be fazed. But if she ever put someone in a book again she would, she vowed grimly, take the trouble-free route and pick a person who was dead!

When Piers opened the door, she shone a defiantly carefree smile.

'This way,' he said, after greetings had been exchanged, and led the way along the bleached-wood-floored hall and into the living-room.

Suzy looked around. Of generous proportions and with French windows which opened on to a wide balcony overlooking the Thames, the white-carpeted living-room was furnished expensively and with some style. There was a black leather sofa with two matching armchairs, a marble coffee-table, a teak unit which filled one long wall and housed a television, video recorder and music centre. Long lime green and white Thai silk curtains framed the windows, and, thanks to the attentions of a twice-weekly cleaning woman, everything sparkled and shone. Her gaze narrowed. Three years ago, she had thought the room lacked soul—and she had not changed her mind. All right, Piers only used the apartment as a stopping-off point between his frequent trips abroad, but where were the ornaments, the pictures, and all the other personal touches which turned a house into a home? The place possessed so much *potential*, Suzy thought wistfully, and a transformation would be so simple.

For a start, if that sunny balcony were filled with troughs of scarlet geraniums and pink Busy Lizzies and——

Her home improvement ideas came to an abrupt end as it registered that her host was waiting for her to sit down. Perching herself at one end of the huge sofa, Suzy decided from the silence that there was no one else around. No letter-wielding, threat-hurling lawyer—praise be. No Amanda Dundas. Could the actress be busy with work, or had she gone shopping? Whatever the reason, her absence also came as a relief.

Smoothing a hand over the dark curls which grew haphazardly at the nape of his neck, Piers frowned. 'I'll give you your interviews,' he said.

'Yes?' Suzy uttered a startled laugh. 'But why the change of heart?'

He levered his long body into the far corner of the sofa. 'Damage limitation. I've been thinking about the kind of things other people might say, and I've decided that if you're going to write a profile come hell or high water, I'd prefer it to be my version.'

A smile spread itself across her face. 'If you can't beat 'em, join 'em?' she enquired pertly.

'Not exactly,' said Piers. 'You see, there are conditions.'

Her smile vanished. She should have known he wouldn't straightforwardly agree. She ought to have realised his co-operation would come with strings attached.

'Such as?' she demanded.

'The first is that I want to take a look at the profile before you submit it to your publishers.'

Her eyes flashed blue sparks. 'You're demanding editorial control? You want to tamper with my manuscript?' she protested, her voice rising in proprietorial indignation. 'But I've already told you that I shan't be overly intrusive, so you have nothing to worry about.'

'In that case, you have nothing to worry about either,' Piers replied, then added stingingly, 'However, you have deceived me once before.'

Suzy's teeth ground together. Compared to his, her deception had been small, and yet he had the audacity to brand her as the villian of the piece! How dared he? Should she defend herself and, no matter how embarrassing it would be, spell out the truth about the past? Should she make it plain that it was *he* who had been the guilty party?

For a moment or two she struggled with all manner of complicated emotions, but decided against it.

'If you're worried about some personal opinions finding their way in, I assure you—yet again—that they won't,' she said glacially. 'Whatever my feelings, when I write I do so from a neutral stance.'

'And I assure you that I shan't tamper, as you call it, unless I consider tampering is necessary,' Piers responded.

A wisp of blonde hair was twisted thoughtfully around her finger. There could be no objection to him simply reading the profile. However, if he wanted to make changes... But first things first. Wasn't the essential thing to have him talk to her, get the piece written—and then bother about any wrangles? After all, once the profile was in hard copy she would be nine-tenths there and in a far stronger position to argue. A fierce light shone in her eyes. And she would argue. She would fight tooth and nail against any interference.

'Done,' she agreed tersely.

'Condition number two,' said Piers. 'For every hour I spend talking to you, I'd like you to reciprocate by spending an hour talking to me; and bring me up to date on what's been happening in the world.'

'You want to fill in the year's gap you have in your knowledge?'

He nodded. 'I thought I'd be able to do it by reading, but after a couple of sessions in the archives room at *The View*, wading through a year's worth of newspapers is already shaping up to be one hell of a slog.' He grimaced. 'Also I find that being faced with so many written words makes it difficult to absorb the facts. However, I figure that if I use the newspapers as a reference point and we discuss events, I'd have a far better chance of taking things in. And as you write articles on current affairs, you must have as good a grasp as anyone.'

'I guess so,' Suzy acknowledged.

'Plus you'd be able to alert me to some of the smaller things which I might miss, like the death of a well-known person or a law which has been passed.' He rested the desert-booted ankle of one leg on the denimmed knee of the other. 'How about it?'

She nodded. 'OK.'

'The third, and final, condition is that during the period while we're talking, which I estimate will take around three weeks, you live here.'

Her eyes flew wide with shock. 'Live here?' she protested. 'In this apartment, with you?'

'That's what I said.'

She stared at him. There had been a time when, if Piers had made such a suggestion, she would have had her suitcase packed and been on his doorstep within the hour—but not now. No, thanks. Not a chance! Suzy's brow puckered. Yet if the idea held no appeal for her, there must—surely?—be someone else who was not exactly jumping for joy over it either.

' "Two's company and three's a crowd" may be a cliché, but you're not expecting me to play gooseberry to a pair of lovebirds?' she protested. 'And even if I was prepared to make up a third, what's Amanda's reaction to having another woman around?' Suzy asked curiously.

'Amanda? You think she's living here?' Piers shook his head. 'She's not.'

'Oh.'

She had taken his girlfriend's residency for granted, but maybe expecting Piers to jump straight back into a live-in relationship was a little premature? Perhaps he needed time to adjust? After all, no matter how resilient he might be, the culture shock between captivity and freedom was severe. It could also be possible that he and Amanda Dundas had not cohabited prior to him being taken hostage. The only thing she really knew about their affair was that it had been in full swing three years ago. Indeed, until the actress had issued her Press statement she had not been aware that it had continued, and, in view of Piers' track record and short attention-span, she had been surprised.

'You haven't found an alternative flat?' he enquired.

'Not yet.'

'So moving in would solve your problem of where to live in the immediate future. This is a large three-bedroomed apartment,' Piers told her, stretching his arms out wide, 'and there's ample space for all your possessions.'

'Maybe, but——'

Suzy broke off to frown. Why was he making the suggestion? One thing was for certain, it could not be out of kindness of his heart!

'My decision to ask you to stay has been made above the waist,' Piers said.

'Sorry?'

'If you're thinking that I might be tempted to leap on you in an impassioned frenzy, don't.' Cool grey eyes met hers. 'While I may have gone a full twelve months without female company, it's not my style.'

Suzy coloured, fully aware that the insinuation was that it was *hers*.

'No, no,' she mumbled.

'It would be a purely practical working arrangement. You're wondering if your boyfriend will raise objections?' Piers enquired, when she continued to frown.

'Boyfriend?' Suzy echoed blankly, then covered her mistake with a laugh. 'Oh, no, he won't mind.'

'So we have a deal?'

While there was no denying that moving into his apartment would give her a much-needed and perfectly timed breathing space in the search for suitable accommodation, she rebelled against co-habiting, albeit briefly, with a man who had once caused her so much heartache.

'Our talking can be accomplished during the daytime,' she protested. 'There's no necessity for me to actually live here.'

'On the contrary, there's every necessity,' Piers corrected, '*if* you want to write a profile that's halfway decent.'

'But——'

'As well as me refusing to talk to you, we both know that all I need do is ring round the people I figure you'll approach and ask them to keep quiet too, and they will,' he drawled. 'OK, if you smile sweetly enough you could tempt a few minds to change, but a word circulated saying how hurt and angry I'd be at any interviews would soon change them back again.'

'You'd do that if I don't agree?' Suzy demanded. 'You'd eliminate my information sources?'

'Every single one,' he said silkily.

'So, in reality, you're ordering me to move in,' she declared, glaring at him along the length of the sofa.

Piers shook his head. 'You have a choice.'

'Some choice!' Suzy retorted.

While she could have managed—just—without him telling her his personal story, it would be impossible to write a rounded profile which would fit in with the others in her book without *some* original statements and observations.

'I don't understand your hostility,' he said, and his grey eyes met hers in a challenging look. 'Could it be that you're afraid living here might revive the strong physical attraction you used to feel for me?'

She glowered. He made it sound one-way, but, in fact, the physical attraction had been very much a two-way thing. It was the emotional input which had come from just one of them—her.

'There's no question of that,' she said stonily.

'Well, then——?'

Suzy turned the matter over in her mind. There were two factors to consider in whether or not she took up temporary residence—her personal preferences and the profile. But which, in the long-term view, was the most important?

'All right, I'll move in,' she said. 'However, I have a condition too; that I pay rent.'

Piers shook his head. 'No need. My salary's high and it's been backing up over the past year.'

'I won't accept your charity,' she persisted, determined not to be placed under any possible kind of obligation.

A dark brow lifted. 'You refuse to be a kept woman?'

'I do. I can only afford what I'm currently paying, which——'

'Whatever it is, it'll be fine,' he cut in, and rose to his feet. 'Let's go and get your gear.'

'Now? You want me to move in today?' Suzy said, in astonishment.

'Might as well. We can ferry everything over in my car.' Piers walked to the door. 'Let's go.'

'I thought you said your collection of worldly goods was modest?' demanded Piers, as he manoeuvred himself into the lift.

It was early evening and he carried a large and widely spreading Swiss cheese plant in one arm and a life-sized ceramic beagle in the other. His brow was sleeked with sweat and there were damp patches on the front of his shirt and between his shoulderblades. For the past three hours they had been hauling Suzy's possessions down from her flat, putting them in the car, motoring over the river, carrying everything from the car and up into his apartment. Again, and again, and again.

She readjusted her grip on two bulky bean-bags which were threatening to fall.

'It is modest,' she protested, secretly thinking that, until now, she had never realised just how many items she had assembled.

'Huh! You have enough framed prints to fill an art gallery, enough——'

'We've done the last journey and this is the final trip up,' she interrupted impatiently and, finding a spare finger, pressed the button. As the lift began to rise, Suzy glanced at the camera which was slung over her shoulder. 'The photographs which your father supplied don't include anything since your return, so would you mind if I took a snap or two some time?'

'You want me to pose in my best bib and tucker?' Piers enquired, peering out from the jungle of dark green foliage.

Suzy recalled his distaste for putting on a tie and jacket, let alone a suit. 'Is that the edge of hysteria I hear in your voice?' she asked sassily. 'Don't worry, a casual shot will be fine.'

He nodded. 'OK. I'll put this plant in the living-room,' he said, as they entered the apartment, 'and, as your room's just about reached bursting point, the dog and the bean-bags had better go in the spare room.'

'Wherever,' she agreed.

Going ahead of him, Suzy set down her cargo beside an intriguing collection of cardboard boxes. Of all shapes and sizes, they bore airline stickers and labels in a variety of different languages. Peering into one which was open, she saw a beautiful green onyx toucan resting among styrofoam pebbles.

'Those are souvenirs which I've collected on my travels,' Piers explained, when he joined her.

'And you've never unpacked them?' she protested.

'Didn't have the time.' He frowned. 'For years I don't seem to have had much time for anything, apart from work. My father mentioned that the two of you were friends,' he remarked, as he offloaded the beagle. He cast her a sideways glance. 'He hasn't been . . . wooing you?'

Suzy burst out laughing. 'Hugo's almost old enough to be my grandfather, let alone my father!' she protested.

'So?'

'He's devoted to Barbara, and I'd guarantee that he's faithful.'

At her assertion, Piers grinned. 'When I was held hostage I kept wondering if their association had continued,' he said, 'and it was good to discover that it had. Barbara's by far the nicest of any of his women, and I like her. We get on well.'

'Couldn't you think again about Hugo's party?' Suzy asked, using the opportunity to make an appeal. 'If you went it would please him so much, and he deserves to be pleased. In order to concentrate on your campaign, he turned down roles in at least two high-profile plays and——'

'My father refused parts because of me?' he broke in, in disbelief.

'Didn't you know?'

Piers shook his head.

'He agrees that you have ample cause to complain about his behaviour in the past,' Suzy went on, 'and he doesn't blame you for rejecting him, but——'

'Hugo's discussed our relationship with you?' he interrupted curtly.

'He mentioned it once, and then only because he was off guard and upset. Upset about you being kidnapped,' she explained earnestly. 'When I went to see him the next day, he seemed to have aged ten years. Your father's usually so full of . . . bombast, but then he was broken. Broken and sad and——'

'You can save the sob story,' rasped Piers, and turned on his heel. 'I'm going to have a shower.'

As he disappeared, a coldness settled around Suzy's heart. His antipathy towards his father might be understandable, but did it have to be eternal? Suzy sighed. Maybe it was because she came from a happy family, but she longed for everyone else's family life to be happy too.

With a burgundy and white-quilted queen-sized bed, white carpet and matt black dressing-table, the bedroom which had been designated as hers had the same impersonal feel as the living-room. Yet, like the living-room, it was luxurious. Mirrored wardrobes filled an entire wall, and after her small flat it was bliss to have so much space for her clothes. As she started to unpack, she cast an admiring glance towards the en-suite bathroom. Tiled in whisper-grey, it had roomy cupboards and surfaces where she could keep her toiletries.

Suzy had not bothered to close the door, and, as she was walking back and forth to the wardrobes, Piers appeared in the hallway. His feet were bare, and all he wore was a white towel fastened low around his hips. A pulse like a second heart began to beat in her throat. He might not have seen a woman for a year, but it was a long time—a very long time—since she had seen a man wearing so little. A man with broad shoulders, a flat stomach, lean hips. A man whose torso was firm, with well-defined muscles. A man covered in golden skin which gleamed with the sheen of good health.

Piers came towards her. 'I have something for you,' he said, and held out his hand.

'My tape!' Suzy exclaimed, in surprise.

'After listening to it, I realise there's not one phrase you'd use.'

She nodded. 'Much too purple.'

'Vermilion,' he said, and grinned.

Time seemed to retreat . . . and stand still. When Piers grinned, the vertical creases on either side of his mouth deepened and his lips curved in a sensual stretch. Once she had traced a fingertip along those creases and around the outline of his lips, Suzy remembered. Once she had licked around his lips and then pushed her tongue deep into his mouth, and . . . What *was* she thinking about?

'Thanks,' she said, and took the tape from him.

As he disappeared again, she returned to her unpacking. Piers Armstrong was her ex-lover, and she had always regarded the 'ex' as short for extraneous, exterminated, *extinct*. Lingerie was thrust into a drawer. Shoes were lined up in the wardrobe. She still did.

Two suitcases had been emptied when she heard the pad of footsteps. Suzy looked up. Once again, Piers stood in the hallway. This time he must have stepped beneath the shower but then stepped out again, for his dark hair was plastered damply to his head and wetness sheened his torso. Diamond droplets sparkled among the whorls of brown-black hair which covered his chest and arrowed down over the flat plane of his belly to disappear beneath the towel. As she gazed at him, her pulses, which had started to race again, broke into a gallop. The breath seemed to squeeze from her lungs.

'What—what do you want?' she demanded, alarmed by the intensity of her responses.

Piers strolled into the room. 'I don't suppose you have any shampoo? I've run out.'

'Yes, I do, somewhere.'

A pile of plastic carrier bags were dumped on the bed, and Suzy began searching feverishly through. She had found the shampoo when, in the corner of her eye, she noticed her camera. If Piers insisted on displaying himself in a state of undress, she might as well take advantage of a photo-opportunity which would have Randolph Gardener cheering, she thought defiantly. Picking up the self-focusing camera, she swung it in his direction. Her finger was pushing down on the lozenge when the figure in the viewfinder unhooked his towel.

Click.

As she lowered the camera, Suzy locked her eyes to his. There her gaze stayed, though it was impossible to ignore the bare bronzed male body which, even in peripheral vision, was making her heart thump like a jackhammer.

'What——' Her mouth had gone dry and she heard herself croak. Clearing her throat, she tried again. 'What did you do that for?' she enquired.

'You said you wanted a casual picture.'

'I didn't want you naked!'

'And neither do I want to appear in your book looking like a sex symbol,' Piers retorted.

How could he be so at ease with his nudity, so uncaring of the towel which hung loosely in his hand? Suzy wondered. She gulped in a breath. She must be at ease too. She would not—repeat *not*—become unglued.

'It may have escaped your attention, but you're already up to your neck in fans who think you are,' she said, her tone painstakingly level and matter-of-fact. 'In fact, half the population of this country appears to either want to mother you or marry you.'

'Which category do you fall into?' he enquired.

'I'm the exception which proves the rule,' Suzy told him crisply, 'I'd like to murder you.'

'That's a bit drastic,' Piers protested.

'Well, how am I supposed to take this film to be developed?' she demanded.

His mouth tweaked. 'With great aplomb. Tell me,' he went on, the amusement growing on his lips, 'what is it you fear should you risk a downward glance? Falling in a dead faint or throwing a fit and rushing screaming from the room?'

Crimson patches of colour bloomed on her cheeks. 'Here's the shampoo,' she said, and thrust it out at arm's length.

Piers laughed, and at last, and to her overwhelming relief, reknotted the towel around his hips.

'Thanks,' he said, taking the bottle from her.

Alone again, Suzy returned to her unpacking. Don't let Piers decide he needs conditioner, she begged, in a silent prayer. *Please*. However, when he next appeared in the hallway he was dressed in a fresh short-sleeved shirt and Levis. His hair was combed sleekly back from his brow and his jaw was newly shaven.

'What would you like for dinner?' he asked, as he directed her into the kitchen. Opening the fridge built in amongst the pine units, he indicated a number of deluxe ready-made meals. 'There's chicken tikka masala, or plaice with mushrooms, or prawn rogan josh or——'

'Prawn rogan josh sounds good. I didn't realise you'd be so organised on the food front,' Suzy remarked, as he cooked rice and deftly chopped the bananas, apples and cucumber which would accompany the curry.

'Being able to rustle up a meal at a moment's notice is one of my two hidden talents,' said Piers, and cast her a glance. 'I don't need to tell you what the other one is, do I?'

She concentrated on setting the table, and said nothing.

The prawns were placed in the microwave and, as the minutes ticked away, Piers removed the cooked rice from the hob and started to drain it.

'Damn!' he complained, when the doorbell suddenly rang.

'Shall I go?' Suzy offered.

'Please. So far the Press have obliged and left me alone, but if this should be a rogue reporter perhaps you'd explain that I'm no longer available for statements.'

Walking along the hall, Suzy composed a polite refusal, but when she opened the door the words stayed in her mouth. Her nerves jiggled. The visitor was a woman in her mid-thirties. She wore a hot orange skinny-rib dress, perilously high heels, and had long straight chestnut-brown hair which hung in a shiny waterfall down to her waist. An aura of showbizzy glamour shone all around her. It was Amanda Dundas.

Suzy pinned on a smile. 'Hello,' she said.

Kohl-rimmed eyes swept up and down her, and the porcelain smooth brow crinkled. Did this indicate recognition? she wondered. Was the actress remembering how they had met before? But the frown seemed to be due to bewilderment—and some irritation—at finding another female on what she plainly regarded as her territory.

'Hi there,' Amanda replied, the supercilious curl of her lip advising that, in any competition stakes, this shiny-faced creature in the crumpled cotton jumpsuit could be dismissed as an also-ran. 'Piers, *darling!*' she called, and swept past into the hall, leaving a heady cloud of perfume in her wake.

'He's in the kitchen,' muttered Suzy.

Wishing, maliciously, that the actress's high-heeled foot would slip on the polished floor and transform her haughty march into a clumsy windmilling skid, she closed the door. Was this her cue to disappear into her bedroom? she wondered. Disappearing would be less trying on the nerves, for, although it seemed ridiculous after all this time, Amanda's arrival had set her on edge. Suzy frowned. His girlfriend might not live with Piers, but that did not mean she would not spend a lot of time at the apartment. So was she doomed to play gooseberry, after all? The prospect brought a shudder, but then she squared her shoulders. Amanda Dundas's presence was something she would need to get used to. Suzy strode back along the hall. Forget disappearing. She was in Piers' home as a *bona fide* guest—albeit an unwilling one— and had every right to join him and his girlfriend. Besides which, her dinner was waiting, and she was hungry.

From the kitchen there came sounds of the new arrival cooing a loving greeting, and when she entered she found Piers with pearlised amber lipstick plastered around his mouth and Amanda draped all over him.

'You don't know each other,' he said, swiftly disentangling himself. 'Suzy, may I introduce Amanda Dundas.'

'How do you do,' Suzy said politely.

'Amanda, this is Suzy Collier.'

The brunette allowed her a brief nod, then swung back to smile at Piers. The impression given, and doubtless intended, was that the two of them inhabited a private world from which Suzy was firmly excluded.

'As I'd begun to tell you, darling,' Amanda said, smoothing a hand over her hip in a way which drew attention to a curve exercised into sleek perfection, 'although you may not have felt able to go out and about while you were at the clinic, I'm convinced it'd be healthy for you to do so now. You need social stimulation, more contact with the outside world. So I've booked us a table at the Café Topaz for eight-thirty. The Topaz is a restaurant-cum-nightclub and it's the "in" place to go,' she informed him. 'The last time I was there, I sat in a booth next to——'

Piers indicated the two steaming plates on the table.

'I'm sorry,' he said regretfully.

'You can tip yours away,' the actress declared, tossing back her waterfall of chestnut-brown hair.

He shook his head.

'All right, sweetie, eat it,' she said, with an indulgent crinkle of her nose, 'and then we'll go out.'

'No,' said Piers.

'Why not?' Amanda demanded, a trifle petulantly.

'One, because at the moment I feel uneasy about being with people in a confined space and, two, because it would be impolite to leave my house guest here on her own.'

'I don't mind,' Suzy assured him.

Piers smiled at Amanda. 'On this occasion, I'm afraid I'll have to take a rain check.'

Suzy shot him a look. If claustrophobia was not an issue—and she had yet to be convinced—then her host was turning down a date with his girlfriend on her account. But his claim of discourtesy had not rung true, so exactly *why* was he reluctant to leave her alone?

'You're staying here?' demanded Amanda, swivelling to frown at her.

Suzy nodded. 'For three weeks.'

Invisible icicles formed in the air and the actress
subjected her to a second inspection, which was closer,
more analytical and decidedly unfriendly.

'It's a business arrangement,' Piers explained.
'Suzy's interviewing me for a book on hostages which
she's writing.'

The chestnut hair was swung back so vigorously,
Amanda seemed to be in danger of dislocating her
neck. Suzy wished she would.

'You need to live here in order to do that?' she enquired, her tone making it clear that Suzy was a low-
life who had conned Piers into the arrangement by
the most underhand means.

'No, but——'

'Perhaps you'd like to join us for dinner, Amanda?'
Piers suggested. 'I dare say it'll stretch to three.'

The brunette peered down at the prawns as though
she would require to be force-fed in order to eat one.

'No, thanks,' she replied, and in a blatant statement
of possession adjusted the shoulder seam of his shirt.
'I'm sure you'll feel ready to mix by next week, so
perhaps we could go to the Café Topaz then?' she
added, adopting a coaxing, wheedling demeanour
which involved much fluttering of her lashes, and
which made Suzy cringe.

Piers smiled. 'Why not?' he said, and shepherded
her out into the hall.

There was a short hushed conversation, then the
front door closed. When he returned, amber imprints
around his mouth gave evidence of yet more kisses.

Suzy eyed them impatiently. For a man who displayed such insight in everything he wrote, he was remarkably obtuse when it came to Amanda. The evening out had not been for his benefit, but for hers. Since their airport reunion, the actress's exposure to the media had been nil, but the *paparazzi* swarmed around the Café Topaz and would have rushed to snap their presence. She did not know what Piers saw in the woman, Suzy thought waspishly, then frowned. Yes, she did. He saw an exceptionally pretty and vivacious brunette, who dripped adoration and who delighted in wrapping herself around him.

'Thanks for that vote of no confidence,' she said, as Piers joined her at the table. 'You think I don't know the real reason why you refused to accompany Amanda?'

He frowned. 'Tell me.'

'You were afraid that if you left her alone, the "Sneak of the Year"——' the repetition of his phrase was frigid '—would take the opportunity to snoop around. I wouldn't. Contrary to what you may believe, I do have principles, and I would never violate the privacy of someone else's home.'

'Glad to hear it,' said Piers. He picked up his knife and fork. 'And now, if you're not planning to throw this food at me, suppose we eat it?'

The curry was good, and so was the chocolate chip ice-cream which they had for dessert. As her host talked about the mementoes which he intended to unpack and of how, after five years, he had finally found time to chat with his neighbours, Suzy's anger subsided.

They had finished the meal and were drinking coffee, when the telephone rang. Piers went through to the study to answer it.

'Is something the matter?' asked Suzy, when he returned, for he looked troubled.

'It's Ed—Edmund Doyle, my fellow hostage. He found our year of captivity hard to handle, and now he's having difficulty coping with civilisation again.'

'Edmund rang now?' she protested. 'But he lives in New York, and it must be the middle of the night there!'

'Sure, but I've told him to call whenever he's feeling down, and at the moment that seems to be any time.'

Suzy remembered the articles she had read. 'The two of you were friends before you were kidnapped,' she said.

'Yes, because we both cover war, though from different sides of the Atlantic, we'd been meeting up for years in various trouble spots of the world.' Piers smiled. 'Apart from that, we have nothing in common—Ed's in his late forties, a widower with two teenage sons—and yet we've always got on well.'

'If I set up my tape recorder, will you tell me about your relationship with Edmund Doyle?' she enquired.

'Now?' he protested.

'Why not? After all, there's only one reason why I'm here in your apartment, and that's to work,' Suzy said crisply.

CHAPTER FOUR

TEN days down and another ten to go, Suzy thought, as she swung the sports car into Piers' allotted space in the apartments' basement parking area. Halfway through. She cut the engine and fixed the handbrake. Yet although the days were being counted off, the reality of living with her ex-lover had turned out to be surprisingly painless. Piers was both an informal host and a generous one. Not only had she been given free run of his apartment—he insisted that the fridge, the drinks cabinet, the telephone et cetera must be regarded as her own—he had also tossed over a spare key and told her to use his car whenever she wanted. But, most importantly for her peace of mind, ever since the photo-opportunity incident he had kept all his clothes *on* in her presence.

Suzy climbed from the car. While she had moved in under pressure and her mind was not *that* peaceful, she could have co-existed in relative contentment with Piers—if it had not been for Amanda Dundas. The actress was the reason for her impatience to leave. Every day, she sashayed into the apartment in a movie queen outfit, a positive fug of perfume and with reams of shiny hair swinging down her back. At which point, any interviewing or discussion of news events was forced to a stop, because now Piers was monopolised. Amanda kissed him. She caressed him. She entwined herself around him like ivy; the poisonous type, Suzy

thought. Thankfully, Piers did not respond in kind—
if anything he seemed irritated to be drawn into such
a performance in her presence—but his girlfriend was
lovey-dovey regardless. She laid it on thick—smile,
smile, charm, charm. Suzy slammed the car door shut.
How could anyone be so perfectly turned out—and
so damned sure of herself?

The first time Ms Gorgeous had appeared on the
scene she had, Suzy recalled, sat around like a spare
part waiting for her to sashay out again. However, on
the second occasion the hint which had been being
flashed from the doe eyes with all the ferocity of a
sawn-off shotgun was taken. If they would excuse her,
Suzy had said, there was some dry-cleaning she must
hand in to the cleaners. And on subsequent days, she
had needed to call at the estate agents—a suitable flat
remained elusive—or shop, or do some research for
her monthly article. Although she resented being
hounded out, she made sure she was gone for at least
an hour. What happened during her absences, she did
not know—nor was she the least bit interested, she
thought, marching across the basement. Her expression became pensive. What she did know was that
Piers continued to refuse all Amanda's exhortations
that they go out—which made her wonder whether
she had been wrong and his fear of crowds was real.

As usual when she let herself into the apartment,
Suzy did so noisily. She dreaded walking in on an embarrassing situation, but so far, each time when she
had returned Amanda had gone. It was the same
today. When Piers called from the study and she went
to join him, he was alone—though the perfume which

clung to him was a cloying reminder of the actress's presence.

'While you were out, one of your estate agents called,' said Piers, as Suzy sat down at the desk and set up her tape recorder. 'He had details of a flat which he thought might be of interest, but I told him it was too small.'

She shot him a disgruntled look. How did he know what might, or might not, suit her?

'Tomorrow Amanda starts rehearsals for a TV sit-com pilot,' he went on, 'so she won't be around for a while.' He cupped a hand to his ear. 'Do I hear a resounding three cheers?'

In truth, this news made her feel like singing and turning cartwheels as well, though it would not be politic to tell him.

'Three cheers?' she repeated, as if at a loss.

'You don't seem entirely *simpatica* with Amanda,' Piers remarked.

Simpatica? The woman was like fingernails on a blackboard to her!

'Her visits have meant that work on my profile hasn't progressed as fast as I'd hoped,' Suzy told him stiffly, 'and I've found it a little irritating.'

Amusement played around the edges of Piers' mouth. 'Only a little?'

She leafed rapidly through her notebook. 'Shall we make a start?'

He opened his mouth to say something—about Amanda?—but then frowned and pulled back as though in danger of violating some unwritten law.

'Yes, ma'am,' he agreed.

*   *   *

Some time in the middle of the night, a noise awoke her. At least, Suzy thought it had been a noise. Drowsily she listened, but when the only sound she could hear was the ticking of her alarm clock she decided she must have been mistaken. Yawning, she drew the covers up around her. She had begun to drift back off to sleep when a noise came again. Suzy sprang alert. Piers had called out something; something which she could not decipher. But why should he call out? The finger of fear tip-tapped its way down her spine. The apartment seemed secure, but there had been a spate of local burglaries, so could someone have broken in and was his call an attempt to warn her?

Lifting her head from the pillow, Suzy strained to hear. There was no pad of footsteps, no voices, no bumps—now no sound of anything—but Piers' room was another room away. Should she investigate? It seemed sensible. Creeping out of bed, she tiptoed across to the door and eased it open. A furtive peep up and down showed her that the darkened hallway was empty.

'No!' Piers called, distantly but clearly.

His voice was strangled and he had sounded anguished. Suzy's heart pounded. It appeared that there were intruders and they could be threatening him. What did she do? Go to his assistance, or sneak into the study and hope to telephone for the police? She was dithering, when Piers cried out again.

'No!'

Of their own volition, her feet carried her along the hall. She had to provide active help—somehow.

Curling her fingers around the brass handle, she cautiously and quietly opened the door. The room's black shadows were patterned with silver-white beams of moonlight which shone from behind the curtains. Fearfully her eyes circled around, but the only person she could see was Piers. He lay in bed, on his side and turned away from her. The sheet had been pushed down to his waist and he was bare-chested. As she gazed at him, he muttered again and moved, flinging out an arm. Now she could see his face. His expression was tense, as though he battled with invisible demons, and a film of sweat gleamed on his brow. There were no intruders; he was having a nightmare.

Suzy's immediate feeling of relief was followed by a rush of sympathy. Piers might not have fallen to pieces like some of the other hostages, yet his ordeal had still brought him his share of insecurities; even though they were well hidden. But now she understood why he had insisted on her moving into his apartment. That practical working arrangement contained a deeply personal element—he did not want to be alone. A lump lodged in her throat. Maybe she was being sentimental, yet she found the thought of this so-independent man being secretly in need of her help and support very touching.

'You bastards!' Piers muttered savagely.

Her lilac satin nightdress swishing around her ankles, Suzy crossed the room and sat down gently on the edge of the bed. 'Piers, wake up! You're at home. You're safe,' she told him.

When his eyes remained closed and the mutterings continued, she stretched out a hand and smoothed the spikes of dark hair back from the dampness of his brow.

'No one's going to hurt you,' she said softly. 'Not now.'

This time her reassurance seemed to be absorbed and accepted, for, little by little, his tension eased. He fell silent and the lines which had grooved his forehead faded.

His lids lifted. 'Suzy?' he said, looking at her in glazed confusion.

'You were having a bad dream.'

Piers ground the heels of his hands into his eyes. 'I thought I was back in that hut in the jungle,' he muttered.

'Have you dreamt about it before?'

'Once, when I was at the clinic.' He reached out to touch her hand. 'Thanks for galloping to the rescue.'

'That's all right. I know how you must feel.' Suzy sat back. 'No, I don't, but I realise that coming to terms with what happened must be difficult.'

'I'm recovering,' said Piers, and grinned.

'I'm sure you are. Goodnight.'

'Don't go,' he said, as she started to stand up. 'Not just yet.'

The underlying note of appeal in his voice surprised her and, unable to refuse such a request, Suzy sank back down again.

'You don't have to sit like a statue,' Piers protested, as she perched straight-backed on the edge of the bed. He patted the space beside him. 'You can lie down.'

She looked at him in surprise. He expected her to lie next to him? When she was wearing a shoestring-strapped and low-bodiced nightdress, and he was naked to the waist? When the last time they had lain in a bed together was when they had been lovers?

'But...um...I...' Suzy faltered.

'It's a king-sized bed, and there's plenty of room,' said Piers, and yawned.

His yawn changed everything. It made her realise that any sexual element was entirely in her imagination. She had nothing to fear from him, nothing to be wary about. All he wanted was the comforting presence of another human being which would enable him to fall asleep again.

Keeping a careful few inches distant none the less, Suzy stretched out alongside. She gazed up at the ceiling. She would stay for five minutes. The bed springs moved as Piers repositioned himself and settled down again. Time passed, and when his breathing levelled into a steady rhythm she turned to look at him through the shadows. His eyes were closed, his dark lashes fanned on his cheeks. He looked younger and softer. No longer the battle-hardened journalist, but more the little boy. A most appealing little boy. She must go back to her room, Suzy thought. But the bed was cosy, and her limbs felt heavy, and her mind seemed to be drugged...

Slowly she became aware of an arm encircling her waist and a warm body fitted spoonlike against hers. She nestled back into the body and the arm tightened around her. She sighed. It felt good to be held. Good to be held by a man, for the arm was muscular and the body which paralleled hers from shoulders, down torso and legs to her feet, was definitely male. Her eyes shut tight, Suzy lay there beneath the sheet, revelling in the closeness, drifting in a languid contentment. She knew she was dreaming and, somewhere at the back of her mind, it registered that dreams as pleasant as this were rare and she should make the most of it.

A few minutes later, she became restless. She half turned towards the man, and as she did, his arm slithered back across the satin of her nightgown and his hand trailed slowly down over her breast. She sighed again and arched her back, pushing closer, pushing her breast against his hand. She wanted him to caress her—and she wanted to caress him. Raising sleep-slow fingers, she moved them blindly upwards until they grazed against the dream man's chest. His chest was hairy and she felt the coarseness of the hair against her fingertips. It tickled.

'Nice.'

Had she spoken, or had he? Whichever one of them it was, the word sliced into her consciousness and the dream ended. In a confused, jolting moment, Suzy came awake. Her lids rose, her eyes widened. The chest she was caressing belonged to Piers! His eyes were closed and, from the satisfied curve of his mouth, he appeared to be floating in the same sensuous world which she had been inhabiting until a moment ago. She snatched her hand away. She must leave his bed and his room, *now*. Before he woke up and realised what she had been doing, she thought feverishly. And he could wake up at any minute, for the sunshine which filled the room said that it was morning.

Lifting the sheet, Suzy started to slide her legs back towards the edge of the mattress. Slowly. Slowly. She was desperate to hurry, but she dared not disturb him.

'Sweetheart,' muttered Piers, in a low husky voice which sounded as sexy as hell and, stretching out an arm, he wound it around her and drew her into him.

Suzy's heart beat like a drum. She lay as stiff as a board. She would wait for him to move again and then, when his hold on her lessened, slide swiftly out and make her getaway. Time, which seemed like hours but which could only have been minutes, passed by. At last Piers moved a second time—but it was to draw her even closer! As her breasts made contact with his chest, her pulses tripped. When she had twisted towards him she must have twisted out of the top of her nightdress, for her breasts were naked. Naked, and scouring against the curls of coarse dark hair.

To her dismay, she felt her nipples harden and the nerve centre between her legs start to throb. The feel of his flesh, the closeness of him, seemed to have sensitised her entire body. Being held against him was torture. Lying still became an impossibility. Straining away, she began to push gently but firmly against his chest; but as if in reflex Piers' arm tightened around her.

'Stay,' he muttered.

I *mustn't*, Suzy thought, in desperation.

Her pushing had changed into a frantic attempt to break his grip when, all of a sudden and not surprisingly, Piers opened his eyes.

'I can't tell you how much I need to feel a woman close to me,' he murmured, and threading his fingers into the loose blonde tumble of her hair, he pulled her close and kissed her.

Suzy knew she should protest, but as his mouth moved over hers with a fierce sweetness a whirlwind of desire seemed to spiral and snatch her up. Her lips parted and his tongue stroked hers, a plundering invader. Heat flooded through her body, and her breathing quickened. Raising a hand, she twisted her fingers among the strands of thick dark hair on the top of his head and held on tight. When Piers had kissed her three years ago she had done that, she remembered. She could also remember savouring the clean taste of his mouth before, and inhaling the musky salt-scent of his body.

But this isn't three years ago, said a voice in the logical part of her mind. This is *now*. So why are you responding to his kisses so deliriously and so obligingly? Why? Summoning up all her will power, Suzy wrenched her mouth from his. She was set to scramble from the bed, but before she could move Piers raised his hands to her bared breasts.

'No,' she begged. 'Please, no!'

'Please, yes,' he said.

As his fingers brushed across the tautness of her nipples, Suzy shuddered. She knew she was in deep trouble. She wanted to go—she did, she *did*—but his caresses were sapping her resistance. Piers drew her closer and, as she felt the rub of him against her, the blood chased through her veins like quicksilver. He was not just naked to the waist, he was *completely* naked. Oh mercy, Suzy thought despairingly, how do I resist him now?

In the study, the telephone pealed out, and as it shrilled a second time, and a third, she found the strength to pull away.

'The phone's ringing,' she said superfluously.

'Let it ring,' muttered Piers.

'But it could be Ed,' Suzy protested. She tugged round her nightgown and covered herself up. 'You must answer it.'

For five, ten, twenty seconds, he gazed at her in silence, then he frowned and took a deep stabilising breath.

'I guess so,' he said curtly and, pulling on a towelling robe, he disappeared.

While Piers was on the telephone, Suzy showered, dressed and prepared the usual breakfast of orange juice, grapefruit, toast and coffee. Everything was done automatically and without thinking. Only one thought filled her head—what had just happened. Why had it happened? Piers had declared his need to be close to a woman—'a' woman, not specifically her, Suzy recollected, and felt an irrational stab of hurt— but how did she explain her behaviour? She nibbled at a thumbnail. It had been biological, chemical, the result of there being no man in her life. She was a little sex-starved, she told herself, and so was vulnerable... that was all. Wasn't it? She straightened the knives, the teaspoons, checked that the coffee-pot continued to perc. Yes.

When Piers ended the call and returned to his room to dress, Suzy walked through to the living-room. The more she thought about her behaviour, the more alarmingly reckless and nonsensical it seemed. She would think about something else. She must. Her eyes circled around. The positioning of her Swiss cheese plant had made a big improvement to one corner, but the remainder of the room was too bare. What was needed was for Piers to put out his souvenirs, but he had yet to get around to-it. A idea struck. Instead of languishing in the spare room, if her ceramic beagle was placed beside the fireplace it would add a focal point. Suzy had located the dog and was carrying it into the living-room, when she heard Piers walk through to the kitchen. Abruptly putting down the dog, she went to join him. Breakfast time was long overdue.

'You were right, it was Ed on the phone,' Piers told her, as they started to eat.

'How is he?' she asked.

'At first he sounded uptight, but he gradually calmed down. All I do is talk to him about everyday things, yet it seems to help.'

Suzy took a sip of her orange juice. While the photographer's current nervous state echoed that of the other hostages she had spoken to, like Piers he was a veteran of dangerous situations. Like Piers, his career meant he had had frequent experience of danger, turmoil and stress. Yet Ed had taken their captivity so much harder. Why? she wondered. She frowned. Or should the question be—why had Piers coped so much better?

'Ed said he hoped he hadn't called at an inconvenient moment,' Piers went on. His pale grey eyes locked unwaveringly on hers. 'I lied through my teeth and told him no.'

'I was only in your bed because you asked me to stay and I fell asleep,' Suzy said, instantly leaping to the defensive.

'But then you woke up and decided to have your wicked way with me.'

Unsure whether to interpret this as an accusation, a protest, or simply a flippant remark, she concentrated on buttering a piece of toast. 'I was dreaming,' she muttered.

'You weren't dreaming when I kissed you,' said Piers. 'You were wide awake.'

'Half awake. And you stopped me from getting away.'

'Did I? Strange, to me it seemed that you didn't want to get away. To me, it seemed as though you were downright eager to continue.'

'And you weren't?' Suzy attacked back.

'It's only natural that I should be a mass of seething hormones.' Piers looked at her over the rim of his cup. 'What's your excuse?'

Her mind ran around in circles. What could she say? How did she explain away a response which did not make any sense to her and which she now very much regretted? How could she possibly justify her actions?

'I felt sorry for you,' she declared, grabbing a reason out of the air.

'Sorry?' he queried.

'Yes. I mean, you were held captive for a year... without physical love and starved of affection... and you had had a nightmare,' she said, and broke off, knowing that with every word she blundered.

The furious tightening of his face had made it clear that Piers was relating what she was saying now to what she had said to him three years ago. Then she had told him she had made love with him not because of straightforward desire, but for another, more calculating reason.

'So, being blessed with a social conscience, you decided to do your good deed for the day and act as a thumb and a blanket. How kind!' he said stingingly. 'Tell me, do you make a habit of being intimate with all the men you feel sorry for? If so, you must have a busy time, because you were always a pushover in the bleeding hearts department.'

'We—we weren't intimate,' Suzy faltered.

'It was damn near.'

Her colour deepened. There seemed little point in denying that. Indeed, if the telephone had not rung there could be no doubt they would have made love and, once again, she would have given herself to Piers Armstrong. Suzy's head thudded. She heard the ominous roll of drums. So much for being more mature! So much for learning from the past! She must leave his apartment, she decided desperately. The profile information might be only half gathered and her belongings would need to be rehoused, but that did not matter. What mattered was her vulnerability towards him. It was dangerous and could be self-destructive. It made it vital she go. Today.

'You don't sleep with your boyfriend, do you?' Piers demanded.

Suzy gave a silent groan. Why had she ever invented the stupid relationship?

'That's none of your business!' she snapped.

'You don't,' he stated. 'If you were having regular sex you'd never have become so aroused so quickly.' He raked her with a glance. 'But even if you don't sleep with the fellow, you're not so hot on allegiance.'

A burning sense of injustice swamped her. Mr Two-Timer of the past had the nerve to accuse her of a lack of loyalty!

'*I'm* not too hot?' she blazed, furious at his insulting summation. 'What about you?'

'A man who's spent twelve months sublimating his sexual urges is bound to respond when a bare-breasted young woman rubs herself up against him,' drawled Piers, and took another drink of coffee. 'How many lovers have you had since me?'

Her chin thrust forward. 'Dozens.'

'I'm serious,' he rasped.

'And I'm serious when I say that my sex life has nothing whatsoever to do with you!'

Piers studied her in silence. 'There is no boyfriend,' he declared. 'You've been here ten days, yet no man's rung or been in touch.'

For a moment Suzy wondered whether to claim that her mystery partner had gone away on business or on holiday, but decided against it. As she was on the point of announcing her departure, there seemed little point in continuing the charade.

'You're right,' she said, and took a breath. 'I've decided——'

'So you lied to me,' he cut in sharply.

'It was only a white lie,' Suzy protested, 'and——' She broke off. The telephone was ringing again.

When Piers returned from the study a couple of minutes later, she eyed him warily. If he revived the accusation of her lying, what did she say? Should she confess to having had no other lover than him? Should she reveal that while she had gone out with various men over the past three years, her dates had always been casual? But instead of returning to the subject, Piers reported that his father had called.

'He wanted to know how I was getting along and if there was anything he could do for me.'

'That was kind,' said Suzy.

Piers frowned. 'Yes,' he acknowledged.

She shot him a glance. To her, it seemed significant that, despite his hostility, he had never completely severed his links with his father. She set her shoulders. Before she went, she would make a final attempt at their reconciliation.

'Hugo told me that he left your mother because, at that time, having a wife and child seemed too big a drain on his emotional resources,' she said. 'He loved her, he never stopped, but he was going through a bad patch in his career. The parts he was offered were small-scale and although he couldn't bring himself to admit it to her—it seemed too shaming— he'd begun to doubt that he had any talent. He worked himself up into such a state that he felt if he didn't get away and spend time on his own he'd crack.'

'You expect me to sympathise?' Piers demanded, his voice cold and his eyes flinty.

'No, but I expect you to acknowledge that he had his reasons for leaving, no matter how wrong-minded they might have been.' Suzy sighed. 'I'm sorry if you have a problem with this, but—— '

'*I* don't have a problem!'

'Then why not listen to what your father has to say?' she asked. 'I know that every time he's tried to explain his side of the situation, you've walked out, but——'

'I'm walking out now!' snarled Piers, and strode furiously away towards the living-room.

Suzy glared at his retreating back. 'Have you never made mistakes?' she demanded. 'Have you never made a complete mess of things and wished you could turn the clock back and start again? All right, Hugo was a bastard to you when you were young, but that doesn't mean you have to be a bastard to him when he's old. You——'

She stopped. Piers had uttered a startled oath. The next moment she heard a crash which sounded like him falling, and then there was silence.

'*Suzy!*'

Deliberately taking her time, she walked through to the living-room.

'You bellowed, sir?' she enquired, arriving to find him sprawled headlong on the floor.

Piers twisted himself round and struggled up into a sitting position. 'Thanks. Thanks a lot,' he rasped.

'You're blaming me?' Suzy protested. 'If you will stamp off in a rage and slip, it's not——'

'I didn't slip. I tripped over your bloody dog!'

She frowned, realising that she had left the weighty life-sized ornament just inside the door. 'Did you smash it?' she asked, looking anxiously around. She had bought the dog when she was on holiday in Portugal with Jo last year and carried it home with great care.

'No.' He jerked his head to where it lay half hidden behind the sofa. 'The thing's not even chipped.'

Suzy let out a breath of relief. 'Thank goodness! Are you all right?' she queried.

'How nice of you to ask. I was wondering how long it'd take you to get around to it,' Piers rasped, and tentatively moved the fingers on his left hand. 'No, I'm not,' he said, wincing. 'I think I've broken something.'

She shook her head. 'Doubtful.'

'You have medical training?' he demanded.

'Of course not, but——'

'It hurts,' he complained.

Suzy heaved an impatient sigh. For someone with a reputation for toughness, he was making a big fuss over what she felt sure was merely a bump.

'Suppose I drive you to the emergency department at the local hospital and they can check it over?' she suggested. OK, the visit would be a complete waste of time, but it had been *her* dog he had fallen over.

Piers moved his fingers and winced again. 'Least you can do,' he said.

The hospital was only a couple of miles away, and when they arrived the emergency department was empty. A young round-faced nurse in starched white linen wrote down Piers' name, address and details of what had happened, and then, in a high breathy voice, declared that she would personally show him the way to the X-ray department.

'Look after the desk, Pete,' she instructed a dozy-looking orderly, 'while I escort Mr Armstrong.'

'Armstrong? Hey!' said the orderly, recognition slowly dawning. 'Aren't you the guy who——?'

'Was held hostage,' the nurse finished for him. She gazed up at Piers like a puppy yearning to be stroked. 'Yes, he is. X-ray's usually busy around now, so he could be gone for some time,' she warned Suzy, and, already chattering about how delighted she had been to learn of his release, she led her patient out into a corridor.

Left alone, Suzy sat down on a bench to wait. There could be little doubt that she too had once given Piers those sickening puppy-looks, she reflected. She sighed. Three years ago, she had been head over heels in love with Piers Armstrong, but head over heels was the worst possible position from which to see things clearly...

CHAPTER FIVE

THE attraction was instant, and mutual. Suzy had looked across the general office at the man who was being pointed out to her as the newspaper's most highly prized and highly paid journalist, and felt a twinge of excitement behind her ribs. He had looked back at this new recruit to the women's page, and come straight over to ask to be introduced. When, after a smiling, laughing, eyes-lingering-on-eyes conversation, he had invited her to have dinner with him that evening, there had been only one answer. Piers Armstrong was the kind of interesting, intelligent, witty man she had always dreamed of meeting. In the blink of an eye, Suzy had known that he was the man for her.

The office grapevine had wasted no time in informing her that, over the years, her new boyfriend had had several affairs. She did not mind. The stories which circulated about virile and dynamic bachelors were invariably over-amplified and, besides, it would have been odd if the most scrumptious man to stride this earth had managed to reach his thirties without notching up a few conquests.

However, three months later, Suzy could not understand why Piers Armstrong had not begun an affair with her. She wanted him to—oh, how she wanted him to sleep with her! And she knew he felt the same. His desire was evident in the heat of his

kisses, in the way he seemed compelled to touch her—
yet always his urges were controlled and he stopped
short of lovemaking. Why? Another piece of information which the grapevine had provided was that
Suzy was several years younger than the women Piers
had previously dated, and this made her wonder
whether he might be restraining himself in deference
to her youth. While this could be deemed chivalrous,
it was unnecessary. She was all of twenty-three! Or
did Piers think she might be unsure of her feelings?
If so, he was wrong. Very wrong. When she gave
herself to him, it would not be casually. She would
be committing herself body and soul to what was destined to be a devout, long-term relationship. So why
must he hold back? It was agony. An exercise in frustration which made her want to weep and wail and
scream.

When Piers invited her to accompany him to a
newspaper awards dinner, Suzy decided that this could
be the night when they finally tumbled into bed. No,
not could—it *had* to be the night, for by now wanting
him had become an acute physical need, like the need
for water or food or sleep. She scoured the shops and
spent far too much money on a backless white jersey
dress. A siren's dress. The kind of dress she had never
worn before. Next came sun-bed sessions which gave
her skin a honeyed sheen, and she experimented end-
lessly with eye make-up. On the day of the dinner,
Suzy left the office early and spent hours bathing,
shampooing her hair, fixing her face and dressing.
When she inspected the final result in the mirror, she
saw an elegant young temptress who was—please,
please—irresistible.

When Piers arrived to collect her, he gave a low growl of approval.

'I look OK?' she asked, twirling round.

'You look *delectable*,' he assured her.

Suzy laughed. The desire she saw deep in his eyes told her she was hovering on the brink of a personal precipice, and that before the night was over she could be stepping off into scary but delicious space. She also thought he looked pretty delectable himself, for the change from casual clothes to white dinner jacket and black bow tie had transformed him into the suave, debonair, preternaturally dishy man about town.

The dress did everything Suzy had hoped for. Her escort's need to touch her was intensified and, on their way to the hotel, Piers drove with one hand resting on her knee and, when they arrived, kept an arm curled possessively around her. They dined with a group of colleagues in a flower-bedecked ballroom, but the people and surroundings made a one-dimensional backdrop. All either of them could focus on was the other. After the meal came speeches and, in time, Piers was summoned to the stage to be presented with an award for 'Best Despatch of the Year'. When he returned bearing his statuette, everyone at the table offered congratulations, and Suzy put her arms around his neck and kissed him.

'That was nice,' murmured Piers, sitting down beside her again as the clamour subsided and the next category of prize was announced.

'Yes, it was.' She cast him a teasing glance. 'You want another one?'

'Later.'

Beneath the tablecloth, Suzy slipped off her sandal and began to rub her bare foot slowly along his calf.

'You can wait?' she whispered.

'Just.'

Acting on impulse, and surprised by her own brazenness, she placed her hand on his thigh.

'You're sure?'

'Behave yourself,' Piers entreated, in a low husky voice.

Suzy opened sapphire blue eyes. 'I am.'

'You're making it hard for me,' he said, as her hand began to slide upwards.

'I am?' she repeated, but this time the words were a provocative question and her eyes danced.

'You're making it hard for me to sit still,' he murmured, catching hold of her fingers and firmly ending their trek. 'If you're not careful, you'll have me leaping up wild-eyed and dragging you with me beneath this table.'

Suzy grinned. 'What would you do then?'

Piers put his arm around her, his hand resting intimately just below her breast. 'Use your imagination,' he said, and smiled.

It was a smile she could have drowned in.

After the presentations there came dancing, and when he took her in his arms and held her close against the whipcord leanness of his body, Suzy was filled with desire. It felt like a tangible force, and she suffered all the hackneyed symptoms—the fast-beating heart, the breathlessness, the weakening of knees when his eyes met hers. She flirted outrageously with Piers, but by now she was waiting, waiting, waiting for him to take her home.

Eventually, the band played the last waltz. Eventually, they climbed into his sports car. Eventually, they reached her flat. As usual, Piers saw her safely inside and kissed her. It was a hungry kiss, a long kiss, and when he stood back his eyes were dark and sombre.

'Goodnight, Sparky,' he murmured, gazing at her through the shadows.

Suzy's heart contracted, tumbled down. He couldn't walk away—not now. Not after an evening which had vibrated with unspoken promise. Not when she *needed* him; her love to be her lover.

'You don't—don't have to go,' she said chokily.

Piers frowned. He knew what she meant, knew what she was offering—she could see it in his eyes.

'I do,' he said. 'It's past midnight, and I'm catching the morning flight to Lima.'

'Stay for a few minutes,' she appealed.

A nerve pulsed in his temple. 'I mustn't.'

'You must,' Suzy said.

She placed a hand on either side of his head and drew him down to her, then, chasing his mouth with hers when he resisted, she kissed him.

When she pulled back, Piers gazed at her for a long tense moment. 'Dear God, Suzy, how am I supposed to stay away from you?' he said despairingly, and his mouth covered hers and he started kissing her, unrestrainedly and disruptively.

Her heart soared. Her lips tingled. She tasted a faint trace of brandy on his breath.

'This is an incredibly sexy dress,' he muttered, drawing his fingers from her shoulders and down the naked length of her spine to below her waist. 'Though

I don't know why you're bothering to wear any clothes.'

'You'd rather I didn't?' Suzy whispered.

'Much rather,' he said.

She led him through to her bedroom where, in the glow of a bedside lamp, he solemnly undressed her, peeling away the dress and the tiny white silk briefs she wore beneath.

'I've lain awake night after night dreaming of your sweet flesh,' he murmured, his eyes heavy-lidded and languorous as they feasted on the curves of her body, the smooth planes, the pelt of golden hair between her thighs.

'Ditto,' Suzy told him, daringly.

His mouth curved. 'Then are you going to undress me?'

A shyness took hold. She had not expected this.

'If—if you wish,' she stammered. With shaky fingers she unbuttoned his shirt and dropped it aside, then, growing bolder, she ran her hands up over the stipple of dark hair which covered his chest and around over his shoulders to the back of his neck. 'What's the matter?' she asked, when Piers suddenly flinched.

'You touched my bruise.'

'How did that happen?' she asked, as he twisted to show her a large yellow-black stain which spread over one shoulderblade.

'When I was in Nicaragua last week there was an unexpected burst of gunfire which had me and a photographer hitting the ground, and I landed on his camera. Now you take off my trousers,' said Piers.

The blood rushed to her face. 'Your trousers?' she echoed faintly.

'You've never undressed a man before?' he said, with a smile. 'I'll help you.'

When he was naked, he drew her down on to the bed and began to kiss her, to stroke and fondle, until her whole body seemed to throb beneath his fingers. She trembled. A need was gathering inside her, building like a wave which started far out at sea and rolled in towards the land. The wave gathered force and as he feasted at the rosy points of her breasts, it surged and sucked her in, and she became part of it.

Piers straddled her. 'Sweetheart,' he murmured, as his body began to slide into hers, but the endearment was followed by a sharp intake of breath. He pulled back, pushing himself up on his arms to look down at her with stunned eyes. 'You're a virgin,' he said.

'Yes,' she acknowledged.

'But it never occurred to me...I mean I didn't...if I had...oh, hell!' he complained, in confusion.

Suzy gazed up at him. He must not desert her now. He could not withdraw and end all these wonderful sensations. Arching her back, she moved her hips against his.

'Please,' she murmured.

Piers cursed, but passion had carried him too far, and now the slide of flesh against flesh, the heat, the moistness, the need which ached in every fibre of his body, propelled him onwards. He had no choice.

'I'll try to be gentle,' he muttered, and, with a harsh, control-seeking breath, he lowered himself into her again.

As her body swallowed him inch by inch, Suzy tensed. The bluntness of him nudged against the unbroken fold of her flesh, and there was a moment of shock, of short, sharp pain. Again Piers moved, and the wave began to build once more. Dominant and relentless, it swept her up and carried her with it. Now all she knew was intense need, whirling desire.

'Piers!' she gasped, as his thrusts became more fevered.

Then the wave was crashing and breaking, bucking and dipping, carrying her on and on and on...until, spent and replete, it dropped her on the shore.

Later, they made love again. This time Suzy felt no pain, only pure unremitting pleasure.

'I must go now,' murmured Piers, as they lay together afterwards, sated and replete. 'Heaven knows, I want to stay with you, but if I don't I'll miss my plane.' Tenderly, he ran his knuckles along her cheek. 'I'll be thinking about you, Sparky.'

Suzy smiled. 'And I'll be thinking of you too,' she said.

Although her interview with Amanda Dundas did not take place until a few days later, when Suzy arrived at the theatre where they were to meet she was still floating on a cloud of happiness. Piers would be gone for a fortnight, but in the meantime she had her memories to sustain her. Such wonderful memories. The first lovemaking was not supposed to be such a good experience for a woman, but her lover's tenderness, combined with his passion, had ensured that for her it had been ecstasy. And now she was eagerly awaiting his return, for then... Suzy gave a contented smile. The future looked so *promising*.

'Miss Dundas's dressing-room is at the end of the corridor,' the elderly stage-doorkeeper told her, when Suzy explained that she had an appointment. He sniffed. 'Madam may be long on hair, but she's short on talent, if you ask me. Don't know why you're bothering to interview her.'

She was bothering because the TV presenter whom she had been supposed to see had pulled out at the last moment, Suzy thought, as she walked down to the indicated door. And as far as Amanda Dundas's talent was concerned, she agreed with the doorkeeper. The woman might be currently appearing in a West End play, but her career to date had consisted of little more than minor decorative television roles. Indeed, her fame—such as it was—came from being photographed as one of the celebrity rent-a-crowd at this film premiere or that product promotion party. And with her doe eyes, sculpted cheekbones and willowy figure, Amanda Dundas photographed beautifully.

Clad in a violet dress with a split skirt which fell away to reveal a shapely gossamer-stockinged thigh, the actress was waiting. Suzy introduced herself, explained the kind of thing she wanted and started to ask questions. Exhibiting an imperturbable self-obsession, Amanda answered them with much *gravitas* and in mind-boggling detail. She took it for granted that the paper's readers would be riveted by this information on *her* lifestyle. The lifestyle of a woman who believed herself destined to become a star.

'Now I'm going to have a cup of jasmine tea and you must join me,' Amanda Dundas declared, when her recital finally ground to an end.

Suzy had been all set to depart, but a kettle in the corner of the room was being plugged in.

'Thanks,' she said, bemused to find that the actress, whose attitude towards her had been distinctly superior, was being hospitable.

'I suppose that, working at *The View*, you must have come across Piers Armstrong?' Amanda enquired, when she had filled two china beakers.

Suzy blushed and gave what she suspected was a goofy grin. 'Yes, I—I know him quite well.'

'Is that so?' The doe eyes narrowed. 'He's a great guy.'

'You know him too?' asked Suzy, surprised, because Piers had not mentioned the actress.

Though the time they spent together was too short to allow much talk of acquaintances, Suzy reflected, a moment later. And, as the interview had been a stopgap, last-minute arrangement, he had not been aware that she would be seeing Amanda.

'I met him through his father,' her companion explained, arranging her skirt and her legs as if TV cameras were ranged waiting for her signal to roll. 'I know Piers *very* well.'

Suzy sipped her tea. The actress had shown a marked tendency to exaggerate when answering her questions, and she felt sure she must be exaggerating again.

'Piers is so brave,' Amanda continued. 'When he was on his last assignment he was almost killed by sniper fire, but he didn't complain—even though he fell and bruised his shoulder.'

'Bruised his shoulder?' Suzy echoed.

No, Piers did not complain, and it was bewildering to discover that the actress knew about an injury which she had only found out about by accident.

'Bruised it badly. If you could have seen his shoulder last Saturday!' Amanda shuddered. 'Oh, dear!'

'Last Saturday?'

Suzy heard herself repeating parrot fashion again, but last Saturday morning Piers had left for Lima.

'He flew off into the wide blue yonder late afternoon, but I was with him before he went. We managed a little get-together.' The lipsticked mouth was covered by girlishly demure fingers. 'Oops! I'm giving away our secrets. Piers won't like that,' the actress exclaimed, and laughed. 'Still, all this is off the record.'

Suzy struggled to make sense of what she had been told. Piers had said he was leaving early on Saturday, but his flight had not been until the afternoon? And, in the interim, he and Amanda Dundas had had an assignation? A sexual assignation, so the lift of the winged brows had intimated—which appeared to be confirmed by Piers having shed his shirt in order for the woman to have seen his bruise. It must be some kind of a joke, Suzy decided. But there's no reason for Amanda Dundas to joke, her mind argued. A tumble of thoughts spun in her head. Maybe the woman was lying. But why should she lie? What motivation could she have? Try as she might, Suzy was unable to think of anything.

Yet Piers' motive in having an assignation with the actress was not so difficult to work out. Her heart shrank. The cloud of happiness whined away like air from a punctured balloon. He could have been finding life with an ingénue like her a trifle dull, and conducting a parallel romance with a far more worldly woman of nearer his own age would have added excitement.

'Apparently there's some young girl at *The View* who has a bad case of the hots for Piers,' Amanda continued. 'He didn't give me her name or tell me what she does, but she's been throwing herself at him in the most flagrant manner. Perhaps you have some idea of who she could be?'

Suzy's cheeks seemed to catch fire. 'No,' she said.

'Seems the kid's pretty enough, but if it hasn't occurred to her that Piers is way out of her league then obviously she's a bit dim. He needs a woman who's his equal——' the actress glanced at herself in the mirror '—not some starry-eyed juvenile. He was telling me about her and we were laughing. You're sure you can't think who the gauche little creature is?'

Suzy felt sick. 'Certain.' She stood up. 'I have a busy schedule and I must get back to the office,' she rattled off. 'Goodbye.'

Amanda tossed back skeins of long brown hair. 'Bye,' she drawled.

Her mouth quivering out of control and hot tears blurring her eyes, Suzy stumbled on to the street. She had imagined her relationship with Piers to be exclusive, and yet, only hours after he had made love to her, he had been in bed with Amanda Dundas. How *could* he? And how long had he been seeing the actress? A month? Two? All the time he had been seeing her? she wondered wretchedly. She had not noticed any signs of his infidelity, but of course, it had never occurred to her to look. Perhaps sometimes when he had reckoned to be travelling, he had actually been in London, holed up in a love nest with Amanda? Suzy attempted to swallow down the pain which was swelling in her throat. What a fool she had been! She should have known Piers would have other girl-friends. She ought to have realised that, no matter how attentive he might have seemed, she was not the love of his life. Far from it. Yet she loved him. *Had* loved him, she thought, fiercely pushing her feelings into the past tense.

Her shoulders hunched as she fought to suppress a sharp gasping grief. The man she had loved had discussed her with another woman, had laughed about her? Piers and Amanda had made fun? Humiliation twisted like a blade inside her chest. Now it was clear why he had been disinclined to make love to her. He had never intended their relationship to advance, so why complicate matters? Maybe there was some honour in his reticence, but she saw nothing honourable about the way he had strung her along for three months. Strung her along because, presumably, it had flattered his ego to be adored—even if the 'gauche little creature' had overdone it!

Blindly, Suzy pushed her way through the shoppers who thronged the pavement. She had been certain Piers cared, yet now she felt as though she did not know him at all and that everything she had believed about their relationship had only existed in her imagination. Scalding tears were brushed from her eyes.

In making love, she had given him the greatest gift a woman could give to a man—almost forced it upon him!—and made the greatest error of her life. And the fact that she had been a virgin added a bitter dimension to his betrayal. Had he told Amanda how she had decked herself out in that white dress? she wondered, squirming. Had he confessed that she had inveigled him into bed and revealed that she was a sexual novice? Her stomach pitched and tossed. No—please, no. Yet it seemed possible. Piers and the actress occupied a far different world from her, a sophisticated jet-set world where the occasional lapse would be tolerated and would not count. As she had not counted.

In the days which followed, Suzy decided she wanted to kill Piers Armstrong. Slowly. She had always considered herself to be a reasonable, moderate person, and to discover she was capable of such hatred came as a shock. She visualised his return from abroad and lay awake until the early hours each night rehearsing what she would say. One thing was definite—he would never be allowed to ridicule her again!

When Piers telephoned to say he was back and ask if they could meet, she invited him round to her flat. As she opened the door, Suzy's heartbeat quickened. He was smiling and seemed so decent, so honest, so genuinely pleased to see her that, for a moment, she was tempted to dismiss what Amanda Dundas had said as so much unexplained rubbish. But only for a moment.

'Hi, Sparky,' he said, with a grin.

'Hello,' she answered, and, sensing he was about to kiss her, turned away.

Piers frowned. 'Is everything all right?' he asked, as she went to perch on the arm of the sofa.

'Everything's fine,' said Suzy, shining a carefree smile.

'You're well?'

'Fighting fit, and how about you?' she asked. 'Collected any more bruises?'

'None.' He gave her a brief résumé of his trip, then slid his hands into the back pockets of his jeans and stood with legs set apart. 'While I've been away I've been giving a lot of thought to us,' he said gravely. 'It seems to me that we could be in danger of going too fast...and that's unwise.'

Suzy spiked him with a look. She had assumed that he would wish to carry on where they had left off. She might not have been his sexual objective, but she was a sex object, if an unschooled one, and, being a lusty male, he would take advantage of the love-making which she had been offering. Instead, it appeared that he was giving her the elbow. Why? she wondered, in confusion. Had she been an utter failure in bed? Or, after three months, had Piers grown bored with having a child in tow? Whichever, *he* would not terminate their affair, Suzy thought fiercely. Piers might have made a fool of her, but if she were to retain any shred of self-esteem she must end it.

'We're not going anywhere,' she declared, lowering her head and talking fast. 'All I wanted when we went to bed was to be relieved of my virginity. Still being...untouched at twenty-three represents a bad case of arrested development in this day and age.' She gave a trill of diamond-bright laughter. 'It was becoming a drag, so I decided to find a man who'd been around a bit and who knew the sexual score, and——' she raised her eyes to see how she was doing, but the emotion she glimpsed in the depths of his eyes was unreadable '—and I chose you.'

'You slept with me because you needed a stallion?' Piers demanded, and the look on his face could now be recognised as one of acute distaste.

A tight muscle seized her throat, but she had to speak. 'That's right,' she declared, making her voice scrupulously casual and throwaway.

'No one can accuse you of pulling your punches,' he rasped.

'Look, you're skilled in such matters, and I'm grateful. You made it a good experience.'

Snapping his heels together, Piers gave an abrupt bow. 'I always aim to please.'

'It's a compliment,' said Suzy, uncomfortable with his hostility and his sarcasm.

'So it is. Glad I could be of service,' he said, and laughed, the anger draining out of him. 'However, I feel bound to point out that although I lost my virginity at a far earlier age than you, the demands of my career mean that much of the talk which concerns the frequency of my sexual activities can be dismissed as hot air.' He strode over to the door, where he raised a hand in farewell. 'I'll see you around.'

She did not want to see him around, Suzy thought, after he had gone; not even from time to time in the distance at the office. She could not bear it. A decision was reached. For a while now her interest in writing about hemlines and how to combat cellulite had been dwindling, so she would leave *The View*. She would seek out a job as a news reporter with another paper and make a fresh start. And as for her liaison with Piers Armstrong, that would be dismissed as a temporary derangement!

'You must have thought you were never going to see me again,' said Piers.

Jerked from her reverie, Suzy looked up to find him standing before her.

'Sorry?'

'I've been gone for so long. Almost an hour.' He raised a hand bound with elastic strapping. 'You want to know the verdict?'

'Please.'

'I've cracked a bone.'

Suzy gazed at him in dismay. 'Is it serious?' she asked, guilt beginning to gnaw as she recalled how dismissive she had been of any injury.

Piers shook his head. 'The doctor says that so long as my fingers remain immobile and free from pressure for the next ten days or so, it'll soon mend. And I guess I should be thankful for small mercies in that it's my left hand.'

As they made their way back to the car, Suzy frowned. She had been about to leave, but how could she leave when Piers was so newly incapacitated—and when it had been her fault? She cast him a worried look. In addition to his injury, he had fallen with one heck of a bump, so there was a possibility that he could be suffering from delayed shock. Suzy inserted the car key into the lock. Her departure must be postponed until tomorrow. However, if Piers should have another nightmare tonight, she would not be taking so much as one step across the threshold of his room!

'Instead of us working, perhaps you should rest for the remainder of the day?' she suggested, when they arrived back at the apartment.

Piers shook his head. 'I feel fine.'

'Then suppose I make you a drink?'

'What of—hot sweet tea?' He shook his head again. 'I'd rather have a cold beer and go on to the balcony, then you can tell me everything my father told you.'

Suzy gave him a guarded look. 'You really want to know?'

'I do, and I promise not to walk out this time. Having been felled by one of your booby traps, I don't intend to risk another,' he said drily.

In the kitchen, she opened a can of beer for him and a cola for herself, and together they went out into the summer sunshine.

'You said my father reckoned he'd never stopped loving my mother,' Piers prompted, resting back against the wrought-iron balustrade.

Suzy frowned. While he might be prepared to listen, his clipped tone warned that his attitude was not suddenly about to soften. He wanted to hear Hugo's version of events, that was all.

'Yes, he didn't leave because he no longer cared, but because he felt inadequate,' she started slowly. 'And after eighteen months or so, when the offers of more worthwhile roles had begun to rebuild his confidence, he decided to ask her if they could start over again.'

'Start over?' Piers protested.

She nodded. 'He knew it was a lot to expect, but to his great delight your mother was in favour. They arranged to meet to discuss the mechanics of him moving back.' Suzy sighed. 'Unfortunately the meeting never took place, because she was killed on her way there.'

Piers' face took on a brooding quality. 'I wasn't aware of that, though the accident did happen near to where Hugo was living at the time,' he muttered. 'But I wonder why my mother didn't tell me they were going to join forces again?'

'Hugo said that because it was something you'd always hoped for, they decided to keep it as a big surprise. And after she died, he was so broken up that he couldn't bring himself to talk about what had so nearly been.'

'And ever since, at his first reference to the past I've beaten a fast retreat,' Piers said reflectively.

'Hugo also told me that from him leaving your mother to her death, there were no other women,' Suzy went on.

He frowned. 'Strange as it may seem, that could be true. I don't recall any hint of infidelity.' He gave a curt laugh. 'But there were plenty of women after she died. Every time I went home on holiday, there seemed to be a different female dancing attendance. In fact, it was a relief to get back to school where I could rely on everything being the same.'

'That was why Hugo sent you to boarding school. He felt it would provide stability—something he sensed he wouldn't be able to provide.'

Piers gazed out across the river to the far bank, where a trio of fishermen sat beneath the lush green fronds of a willow tree, patiently waiting for a catch. 'He also sent me because having a small boy around would have cramped his style,' he remarked thinly. 'On your tape Hugo said he hadn't been able to give me as much time as he would have liked, but he *chose* not to give me time.'

Suzy bobbed her head in a rueful nod. 'He admitted that. He admitted selfishness played a part.'

'So one month my mother dies and the next I'm shipped off to a place I didn't know, to live among people I didn't know. What a lot of fun that was!'

She flinched. She had heard the rawness of his hurt—a hurt that went straight to her heart.

'You had a rough deal,' she said.

'Maybe, but one thing's for sure, when my turn comes to be a father I shall be a caring one.' He took a brisk swig from his beer. 'Still, being emotionally isolated meant I grew up fast and learned to be self-sufficient from an early age.'

'It also enabled you to cope so well with being held hostage,' said Suzy, in abrupt realisation.

Piers frowned, considering the idea. 'I guess so,' he acknowledged. 'After surviving the sheer desolation of those first months at boarding school, I knew that whatever else life might throw at me it could never be as bad. It wasn't,' he said, and fell silent.

Below on the river, a lone oarsman sculled by, the deft plunk-plunk of his oars spreading rippling circles across the glassy sun-sparkled surface of the water.

'I'll ring my father and tell him to reorganise his party,' said Piers, all of a sudden.

Suzy felt a glow of pleasure. While it would take more than one evening to wipe out the years of disharmony—they might never be completely wiped out—his acquiescence represented a first step in the right direction.

'Great,' she declared, then tilted him a look. 'Claustrophobia won't be a problem?'

Piers watched the oarsman's progress. 'Shouldn't be. Chances are the doors'll be open from the living-room on to the courtyard, so if I feel queasy I can always wander outside.' He swung back to her. 'I'll tell Hugo that while we're there he's to take half an hour off and give you an accurate report of his reactions when I disappeared.'

Suzy smiled. 'Thanks.' It seemed certain that if it was Piers who asked, she would be told the truth. 'When you were held hostage, did you never consider making things up with your father?' she asked.

'Many times.'

'But?'

Piers expelled a sigh. 'But when I was released and we met again, all the old negative feelings seemed to creep back and take over.' He grinned at her. 'What I needed was someone to nag some common sense into me.'

'I didn't nag!' Suzy protested.

'No?'

'I . . . persevered.'

'So that's what it's called,' he said and, tipping back his head, he swallowed down the remains of his beer. 'I'll go and ring my father.'

She had not included herself amongst the guests at the party, Suzy thought, as Piers disappeared, but the opportunity to interview Hugo again was too good to miss—and she knew that he and Barbara would be happy for her to attend.

'We're to be there on Sunday at eight o'clock,' Piers reported, coming back on to the balcony a quarter of an hour later. He grimaced. 'Dressed in our best.'

'This Sunday?' asked Suzy, for it was already Wednesday. 'The party's so soon?'

'It's Hugo's first free evening from the theatre, and he insisted that everything could be arranged in time.' Piers' smile was dry. 'He probably thought he'd better have it in double quick-time, in case I changed my mind. After I'd spoken to him, I rang Ed,' he went on. 'When I was waiting to be X-rayed I got to thinking about the poor fellow, and I decided that if I could join him for a few days it might help boost his spirits and hasten his recovery.'

'I'm sure it would,' she agreed.

'So we've fixed that you and I will fly over to New York on Monday.'

'*Me* fly over?' Suzy protested.

He nodded. 'To stay until Thursday.'

She stared at him, her blue eyes wide. She was expected to accompany Piers to the States? But tomorrow she had planned to get out of his apartment and his life, for ever.

CHAPTER SIX

'YOU'D be able to write about how it is when Ed and I meet up again and include an account in your profile,' Piers said. 'I've told him you'll do an excellent job, and he's happy for you to have the exclusive.'

Suzy's news nose started to twitch and she felt a stirring of professional excitement. An exclusive of such interest was something to kill for, yet she was being offered it on a plate.

'You've read examples of my work?' she asked curiously.

Piers nodded. 'And I like your style. It's lucid, it's reasoned, and you always hit the mark.'

'Thanks,' said Suzy, and was unable to stop a smile because, coming from someone so talented himself, this was praise indeed.

'I'm going to have another beer,' he went on. 'Do you want another cola?'

'Um—please.'

As he disappeared, Suzy curled her hands around the balcony rail. A chance to witness the reunion of the fellow hostages was of mouth-watering appeal to her journalistic instincts. It would make wonderful copy. But... But... All her *personal* instincts told her that the longer she remained in close proximity with Piers, the more at risk she would be. So did she chance the trip? A tug-of-war started up in her mind.

121

'An air ticket to New York costs money,' she said, when Piers returned with their drinks. Taking his can, she ripped off the ring-pull, then did the same with hers. 'Right now, I don't have that kind of money to spare.'

'And you'd rather walk over hot coals than allow me to act as benefactor,' he remarked sardonically. 'Kingdom Publishing will pay. Believe me, they'll be delighted to finance a first-hand account which will send the public flocking to buy your book in droves.'

She did believe him. She swallowed down a mouthful of chilled cola. She was also aware of being manoeuvred—again. As with living in his apartment, there were strong inducements for her to travel with Piers to America, yet she remained the puppet while he pulled the strings. She felt a spasm of impatience. It seemed that whenever he said jump, she invariably leapt ten feet into the air. And yet why, on this occasion, did he want her to jump?

'What do you get out of it if I go to New York?' she demanded, her blue eyes suspicious.

'Do I have to get something?' Piers protested.

'For sure,' she said crisply.

He raised his bandaged hand. 'This means that I shall need someone to cut up my food, tie my shoe laces—' he paused, pale grey eyes meeting hers. '—soap me down when I'm in the shower.'

Alarming scenarios jostled in her head. 'Soap— soap you down?' she faltered.

Piers laughed. 'Just joking—about that. I guess I'll have to soap myself——' he heaved a gusty sigh '—though it won't be easy.'

'So the trade-off is that I'm to be your Girl Friday?' she demanded.

His lips curved. 'I was thinking more in terms of you being my slave.'

'Don't push it,' Suzy warned, and frowned. Even though she was being pressurised, Piers had damaged his hand because he had tripped over the pot dog which *she* had discarded, so accidental or not, much of the responsibility for his current predicament had to lie with her. 'I'll come, but only if Kingdom are willing to pick up the tab,' she said.

'Ring them and see. And ask for a first class ticket.'

'First class?' Suzy queried. She had never travelled first class in her life.

'There's a chance I could be recognised, and if we go first class it'll give me more privacy,' Piers explained.

Kingdom were willing—to pay for her to go first class, to pay for everything. Indeed, when she rang him Randolph Gardener cheerfully informed her that if she would prefer to stay at the Waldorf Astoria rather than at Edmund Doyle's apartment, he was happy to foot the bill.

'It'd be easier for Ed if I did book into a hotel,' Suzy pointed out, when she relayed the telephone call.

'Maybe, but he seemed keen that we should both stay with him,' said Piers, 'so I think we should stick with that.' He swigged from his can. 'Have you visited New York before?'

'No—but you have.'

'Many times, though I was usually passing through on my way to somewhere else, so the airport was as far as I got,' he said, and regretfully explained how, although over the past ten years his job had taken him to most countries in the world, he had never managed much sightseeing.

'Suppose I make dinner for us this evening?' Suzy suggested, as they finished their drinks.

Piers lifted a brow. 'This is your way of ingratiating yourself after being so pitiless when I was in the throes of agony?' he enquired.

'This is my way of saying that, good as your pre-prepared meals are, I'd prefer some home cooking for a change,' she responded. 'Any choices as to the menu?'

'Let's have something special.' He slid her a smile. 'After all, if you're ingratiating yourself you might as well do it in style.'

'How about smoked salmon, followed by grilled fillet steak with garlic butter, baked potatoes and a tossed green salad?' Suzy suggested.

'Sounds great.'

'And for dessert——'

'That pudding with apple underneath and sponge cake on top,' said Piers, when she hesitated, searching for ideas. 'I haven't had it for years, and I love it.'

'Adam and Eve pudding. Will do.' A look at her watch revealed that it was noon. 'I'll go to the supermarket now,' Suzy decided, 'and I'll bring us back a pizza for lunch.'

'And after we've eaten you can start quizzing me again for your profile.'

She gave him a doubtful look. 'You're sure you wouldn't rather rest?'

Piers groaned. 'Nag, nag, nag! I'm positive,' he told her.

Whatever agony he might have gone through, his stamina was not affected, and they worked non-stop throughout the afternoon and into early evening. And then Suzy's questions only ended because the telephone rang and it was Julian Fairlop, the editor of *The View*, at the other end of the line. As Piers started into what seemed destined to be a lengthy conversation, she closed her notebook, switched off her tape recorder and headed for the kitchen. They had worked long enough, and it was high time she started making inroads into dinner.

As she assembled ingredients for the pudding, Suzy recalled seeing Julian Fairlop on television shortly after Piers' release. Smiling with relief, he had praised the manner in which his much-lauded journalist had handled being held hostage and said how honoured he felt that he worked for his paper. And ever since, the editor had maintained a protective, watchful presence in the background.

'I've been offered a new job,' Piers announced, when he eventually came through to the kitchen. Sitting on one corner of the table where she was working, he folded tanned muscled arms. 'As political editor.'

Suzy was whisking eggs, but the beater slowed in her hands. While the position represented a wonderful step up in the newspaper's hierarchy, it would mean far less travelling, far more time spent at base. Most men would have considered this an advantage, but Piers thrived on forever coming and going. He seemed psychologically suited to being footloose and fancy-free. Her brow furrowed. And yet, although the job was very different from his present one, there could be no doubt that he would do it well. His intelligence and energy meant that whatever he did, Piers did well—like making love, a little voice in her head reminded her.

'It'd be one heck of a promotion,' she observed, thinking how most journalists lusted to become an editor.

He nodded. 'The present guy's decided to take early retirement, and so, if I want it, I start in six weeks' time.'

She added the eggs to the creamed butter and sugar, and folded in the flour. 'What did you do—refuse outright, or play diplomat and say you'd sleep on it and call back?' she asked.

'Neither. I accepted.'

Suzy looked at him in blank astonishment. 'You did?'

'Of course. Not only will being political editor dramatically expand my career horizons, but it'll mean a less frenetic existence,' said Piers, and his tone became grave. 'I've never expended much time on navel-gazing, but over the past year I've realised that I need to strike a far better balance between the personal and professional sides of my life.'

'Not be away so much?' she asked, as she placed the pudding in the wall oven.

'Yes. I want to stay home and put down roots.' He frowned at her. 'It's clear to me now that having a loving, intimate relationship is what makes life worthwhile and that, if I want a relationship to be a success, I have to work at it. And to do that, for a start I need to be there.'

Suzy eyed him speculatively through lowered lashes. His distaste for permanency had seemed in-built, but earlier Piers had referred to being a father and now he was talking about relationships, so did this mean he had marriage on his mind? In that case, he would need to split with Amanda Dundas, she thought drily, for there was no way the actress would put her career on the back burner, let alone offer up the body beautiful to pregnancy and the risk of stretch marks.

Though a split would not be so surprising, Suzy mused. While Piers' attitude towards his girlfriend was forever amiable, he did not seem one-hundred-per-cent *struck*. For example, he was not driven to touch Amanda; as he had once been driven to touch her. Nor had she noticed any sharing of jokes or making each other laugh, as there had been with them. *Was* with them—for their days of talking were interspersed with moments of mutual amusement. Suzy switched her mind back to Piers and Amanda. The more she considered a split, the more one seemed imminent.

'Staying put will be a big change,' Suzy remarked.

'But I've changed,' said Piers.

Had he? she wondered. Truly? Permanently? It was easy to see how settling down might appeal to a recently returned hostage, but that appeal could be transitory. Indeed, in a month or two, when his ordeal was further behind him, he might well revert to his usual nomadic, go-it-alone self. Then marriage would become a no-no, and then he might regret having accepted the promotion.

Leaning forward, Piers ran a finger around the inside of the mixing bowl and scooped out a glob of the remains of sponge mixture.

'Good,' he said, tasting it. He stepped towards her, his finger held aloft. 'Would you care for a suck?'

There was something in the depths of his eyes which made her heart flutter and caused the air to vibrate.

'No, thank you,' Suzy answered.

'No, thank you,' echoed Piers, so accurately mimicking her stiff and starchy tone that she was forced to smile. 'You won't pick up some anti-social disease,' he told her.

'I didn't think I would.'

'So?'

His gaze was insistent, trapping her and leaving no way to escape. Sticking out her tongue, Suzy took a tentative lick at the mixture. Her aim was to avoid touching him, but, all of a sudden, he moved and she found herself with his finger inside her mouth.

'Enjoy it,' Piers instructed, as her eyes flew wide with surprise.

Sucking the sugary cream from the solidity of his finger had a disturbing effect. The soft liquid suction, the graze of her tongue over his skin, his knuckle, his nail, seemed heart-bangingly *intimate*. And when she finished and Piers used the same finger to polish out a second glob which he immediately placed in his own mouth, the feeling was intensified. Before he had chance to make a third foray, Suzy grabbed up the bowl and the rest of the baking clutter and dumped them in the sink.

'I'll wash up,' she said.

*   *   *

Although an unexpectedly late departure from Hugo's party allowed them only a scant four hours' sleep, both Suzy and Piers were awake the moment their alarm clocks rang. Suitcases were locked, cups of coffee hastily drunk, and they were outside, ready and waiting, when the prearranged taxi arrived to take them to the airport. At that point they had plenty of time to catch the New York flight, but halfway along the motorway there were roadworks. Three lanes of traffic were forced to merge into one, and in the resulting congestion their taxi stood, travelled a yard or two, and stood again. As the minutes ticked away, Suzy started to fret.

'We shall miss the plane,' she said, peering anxiously ahead at the stop-start queue.

'If we do, we can always take another one,' Piers shrugged, the pragmatic seasoned traveller.

However, now the gods decided to smile. Past the roadworks the M4 was free-moving and, heeding Piers' request, their driver drove in breath-holding, nail-biting Ayrton Senna style. At Heathrow, their sprint to the check-in desk was followed by a dash along what seemed like miles of moving walkways, but they made it—though seconds after boarding the plane door was thudded closed behind them. A steward showed them to their seats, helped stow their hand luggage, then took up his position at the front of the cabin and began to demonstrate the safety procedure. The pointing out of exit routes, et cetera, gave them time to catch their breath.

When the demonstration was over, Piers located the straps of his seatbelt. 'Would you fasten this for me?'

he asked, indicating the buckle that lay across his thighs.

Suzy gave a silent scream of protest. 'Yes, master,' she said lightly, and leant across him.

'You smell nice,' he murmured, brushing aside her hair to inhale the fragrance released from the pulse point below her ear. 'Of lily of the valley, and it's just a trace. Not like Amanda, who douses herself with so much perfume she must annihilate every insect within fifty yards.'

'A hundred yards,' Suzy said smartly, but when she sat back her expression grew thoughtful.

It was unusual for Piers to make any spontaneous reference to his girlfriend, let alone criticise her. While he might talk freely and candidly about his hostage experiences, when it came to the romantic side of his life he was tight-lipped—almost obsessively so. Could his silence mean that ever since his return he had felt uneasy with the relationship? It seemed possible. Suzy frowned. If Piers *had* talked about Amanda, praised and idolised her, she would have found it difficult to listen. Very. Time and again, she had told herself that her attitude towards the woman would be one of cool indifference—why should she let her bother her?— but everything about Amanda irritated beyond belief.

As the jumbo jet reversed ponderously from its stand, Suzy's mind went back to the previous evening and how the actress had rung Hugo to say, sorry, she had been unavoidably delayed, but would be along later. Two guesses had not been needed to know that the delay was deliberate and a grand late 'here I am folks!' entrance was to be staged. Her mouth gave a sudden twitch. But for once, Amanda had miscalculated.

Last night, when she and Piers had arrived, Hugo had graciously, if speedily, accepted their gifts of wine and flowers, and then ordered them to close their eyes. Taking their arms, he had steered them along the hall, until Suzy had guessed they must be standing beneath the archway into the drawing-room. 'You can look now,' he had said, and they had found themselves facing a wall of fifty or so people, all grinning like loons and all bearing champagne glasses raised on high. Barbara had been fronting the assembly and, at her command, everyone had bellowed, 'Welcome home, Piers!' Suzy's lips curved into a soft smile. The moment might have been contrived and theatrical, yet she had found it moving. Hugo had also ensured that they had made an entrance which the actress had had no chance of topping.

However, although her arrival might have gone un-noticed—Amanda had posed for a long moment in the archway, but the guests were busy chatting—she had been extremely noticeable. Suzy scowled. While she had responded to the demand to 'dress in her best' by wearing a gauzy clover-coloured top with matching palazzo trousers, Amanda had dressed to kill. Clad in a silver lace bustier, painted-on silver lycra pants and needle-thin heels, she had looked sickeningly skinny and sickeningly beautiful. A grin took root in the corner of Suzy's mouth. However, while the lycra pants had revealed slender, daily-exercised, mile-long legs, they had also revealed that those legs were bowed—only slightly, but bowed none the less. Bandy Mandy, she thought, and her grin bloomed.

'Amanda's late arrival yesterday meant she missed out on your big welcome,' Suzy could not resist remarking, as the plane waited for take-off at the end of the runway.

'But you shared it with me.' Piers smiled as he recalled her response. 'And salt water welled in her eyes.'

Suzy's chin lifted. 'You were touched too,' she protested.

'I was,' he agreed. 'I owe my father an apology,' he carried on; 'a good three-quarters of the guests were my friends.'

'He must have been on the phone for hours to get everyone there at such short notice.'

'And then he made sure they all had such a great time that the party was still going strong at three a.m.,' Piers reflected.

Suzy grinned. 'Plus he gave me truthful answers to all my questions.'

The mighty engines roared and the jet moved forward, its speed increasing until the nose lifted and they rose up, up, up into the air. When the cruising altitude had been reached, breakfast was silver served. Freshly squeezed orange juice came first, followed by a choice of bacon and eggs or kedgeree, and finally croissants and coffee.

'I'm going to get some shut-eye,' said Piers, when their dishes had been tidied away.

Suzy yawned. 'Me too.'

'Before we settle down, would you help me off with my sweatshirt?' he asked.

She gave another silent scream. 'My pleasure,' she said, and together they eased it over his head.

As Piers tilted back his seat and closed his eyes, Suzy rested back too. By this time next week she would have gone from his apartment, she thought wistfully. The rented flat which he had turned down had been chased up, approved, and a deal agreed. She moved in the day after they returned from the States. Piers might have continued to claim that the place was too small—and perhaps he was right—but she had insisted. She had also insisted that, despite their New York visit, the remaining time they had together was sufficient for her to complete her profile research and bring him up to date on world events. So all she needed to do now was survive the next five days, and she would be free.

Free of being with him morning, noon and night. Free of having to *touch* him. Suzy gazed out at the white cotton-wool clouds which floated in a china blue sky. She was often required to help by, as a moment ago, removing a sweatshirt, or fastening the watch which Piers now wore on his right wrist, or perhaps by cutting a fingernail. All right, these were brief, everyday actions—and Suzy knew that if she had been performing them for anyone else, she would have done so without thinking—but when she did them for him they seemed weighted down with accidental eroticism. So much so that, with each day which passed, she became more nerve-rackingly aware of Piers. Aware of him as a sensual, attractive, desirable man. A man who had not been exterminated from her life nor was extinct, but who continued to have a disturbing *effect*.

Suzy frowned, her thoughts returning, yet again, to the previous evening. As several of the guests had been her friends too, she had decided to concentrate on them and forget about Piers. Some hopes! After interviewing his father, she had joined a group of former colleagues, but had soon found herself wondering how he was coping with the crowd. A surreptitious scan had shown that Piers was not in the drawing-room, so had he done what he had said and gone outside? As the chatter had swung back and forth around her, Suzy had peered towards the courtyard, which was filled with the mauve shadows of twilight. Piers had been there, standing in a secluded corner away from everyone else and with his back towards her. He was talking to Amanda Dundas. From then on, her gaze had seemed magnetically drawn, so she knew that their conversation had continued for the next quarter of an hour—after which time the actress had left.

Suzy nibbled at her lip. Amanda had said she wanted to study her lines for the next day's rehearsals, but to exit just after ten o'clock had seemed extreme. The show was only a sit-com, and her lines could not be that onerous, nor demand that much reflection. Such a premature departure had also been out of character. In addition to being ambitious, Amanda Dundas was what the papers described as 'fun-loving'. This meant that whatever the event, she was invariably in the thick of it and stayed to the bitter end. Suzy adjusted the belt that cinched the waist of the brown chambray slacks she wore now with a white broderie anglaise shirt. She had felt Amanda might not have been giving the real reason for her early and somewhat abrupt departure, and she still had her doubts.

She had also wondered what Piers and his girlfriend had been talking about. At one point he had spoken intently, while Amanda was all nods and rapt attention. Then, in a switch, she had tossed back her glossy hanks of hair, linked an arm through his and launched into a lengthy and intense spiel. At the end, both of them had been smiling. After Amanda's departure, when Piers had come to join her, his mood had been light-hearted, if not edging on the euphoric. He had seemed as though a heavy weight had been lifted from his shoulders.

Her brow creased. Could Piers have been telling Amanda it was goodbye? Had she witnessed a parting of the ways? If so, the actress had taken the news calmly, though of course she would not risk losing face by publicly protesting. On the contrary, it would be typical of her to mask the fact that she had been ditched with wide, wide smiles. For Piers to choose to give Amanda the elbow at the party seemed a little cowardly, Suzy reflected, and she had never considered him to be a coward. But——

A thought hit with a sudden, sickening jolt. Maybe she had got everything back to front. Maybe, instead of prising himself away from Amanda, Piers had been drawing closer. Maybe their discussion had been about marriage! Suzy's mind seemed to shoot off in ten different directions at once. A proposal would fit in with the final smiles, Piers' relief could have been due to him being accepted, and Amanda might have rushed off because she had been eager to break the news to her family. All right, it was difficult to imagine the actress committing herself to domesticity, but she had reached her middle thirties and could have heard the tick of her biological clock. It happened. As for Piers never seeming smitten, that was easily explained by him deliberately playing down his affection in front of her.

Clawed hands seemed to grab hold of Suzy's heart and squeeze it tight. Piers couldn't be such a sap as to marry Amanda! He couldn't wed someone who was so sly, so self-centred, and such a poser! It was unthinkable, wrong. It would be a tragedy. Suzy inhaled a deep and steadying breath. If Piers had asked Amanda Dundas to be his bride, that was his choice. It had nothing to do with her. She did not care. All she cared about was getting through the next five days and getting away from him.

Although it took her a long time, as the plane flew out across the Atlantic Suzy did eventually manage to fall asleep. But her rest was fitful, and when Piers began to stretch and yawn beside her, she immediately came awake to discover that the jet was reaching the end of its long descent into New York's Newark airport.

'The last occasion when I stepped off a plane, I was greeted by a hundred flashbulbs popping and banks of television cameras,' Piers recalled, as he wiped his face with a hot towel. 'But not this time, thank goodness!'

In subsequent telephone calls, he and Edmund Doyle had agreed that their reunion would be kept secret from the media, and so he was arriving in New York anonymously. Suzy had been grateful for this. Despite their working relationship, she was reluctant to be publicly seen with Piers; in case the media mistook her as a replacement for Amanda and bombarded her with questions. And when, as was planned, the two ex-hostages faced newsmen at the end of their stay, she would be keeping well clear.

Edmund's sons, Harv and Jason, were to meet them, and when they emerged into the arrivals hall they saw two teenagers holding aloft a card emblazoned 'Armstrong'. Each boy was stocky and sandy-haired, and each wore black elasticated shorts, baggy T-shirts and back-to-front baseball caps. Introductions were made and Harv, who at eighteen was the elder by two years, immediately commandeered Suzy's suitcase, while his brother carried the one belonging to Piers.

'Pop's real excited about your visit,' Harv remarked, as they made their way through the airport building and out to a massive parking lot.

'How is your father?' Piers enquired. 'He's told me he's finding it hard to acclimatise——'

'Very hard,' the youth cut in. 'He tries to put on a brave face, but the truth is that he's living on his emotions and he's, y'know, like fragile.'

'He needs everything to go smoothly and be perfect,' Jason explained, with a grimace. 'All it takes is some little bitty upset, like if we argue over which TV show we want to watch, and he gets so-o agitated. The psychiatrist told us it'll take a while before he's anchored again and that in the meantime we're to handle him with kid gloves.'

When they reached a large white Buick, the boys stacked their suitcases in the trunk and everyone climbed inside. Harv took the wheel, with his brother alongside, while Piers and Suzy sat in the back.

'I guess you're going to be occupied with Pop all the time you're here?' said Harv, speaking to Piers.

He nodded. 'I expect so.'

The youth grinned at Suzy through the rear-view mirror. 'In that case, maybe I could take you around a bit?' he suggested, as they headed out on to the freeway.

'Maybe *we* could take her around,' Jason corrected, shooting his brother a dirty look.

Harv ignored him. 'How do you fancy a helicopter flight out to the Statue of Liberty?' he enquired, grinning at Suzy again.

She nodded. 'Sounds good.'

'Have you been in a helicopter before?' Jason asked.

'Never.'

'Nor me,' he said, 'but it'll be ace.'

'Should be,' she agreed, and peered ahead.

Across the sparkling blue stretch of what she knew must be the Hudson River, the towers and needles of the Manhattan skyline shimmered in the hazy sunshine. Suzy smiled. The view was so familiar that she found it hard to believe it was for real.

'You're astounded by the resemblance to the New York skyline?' Piers enquired drolly.

She laughed. 'Yes. Look, there's the Empire State Building,' she said, pointing a delighted finger.

'You see the one with the distinctive spire?' Harv said. 'That's the Chrysler Building.'

'The two towers together are the World Trade Center, which is the tallest double skyscraper in the world,' Jason put in, not to be outdone.

As they motored on, dipping down through a tunnel beneath the river and emerging on to the busy, noisy canyon-like streets of Manhattan, their teenage escorts vied to point out the sights. With her blue eyes swivelling from right to left, Suzy caught glimpses of Madison Square Garden, Macy's famous department store and the jam-packed length of Fifth Avenue.

'Now we're in SoHo, which is where we live,' Harv explained, as they reached a neighbourhood brimming with antique shops, art galleries and an endless variety of ethnic restaurants. 'It used to be a warehouse district, but then the artists moved in and made it trendy.'

'So it's one of *the* places to live,' Jason added.

'I know that London's Soho took its name from a hunting cry, but what's the origin of this SoHo?' Suzy enquired.

'It stands for South of Houston,' the boys explained, in unison.

'And Houston's a street,' Piers told her.

'The buildings are amazing,' she said, as the Buick came to a halt outside an apartment block which was lavishly decorated with lacy iron trims and balustrades.

'This is what's known as the Cast-Iron Historic District,' Jason told her. 'I could take you on a guided tour.'

'*We* could take you,' Harv amended.

Suzy grinned. 'I'd like that.'

They were stepping out on to the pavement when a voice from above suddenly shouted, 'Piers! Hey, Piers!' and everyone looked up to see a thick-set man with thinning sandy hair waving wildly from an upper storey balcony.

Piers grinned and waved back. 'Hi, Ed,' he called.

Inside the building, an old-fashioned cage lift carried them slowly and creakily up to the landing where the photographer was waiting. As Piers stepped out, Edmund made a grab and clutched him tight against his chest. For several minutes, they hugged each other.

'There aren't words to express how good it feels to see you again,' the older man mumbled, the tears pouring down his cheeks.

Suzy swallowed hard. Although the journalist side of her was busy taking professional notes, the human side could not help but respond in its usual soft-hearted way. And when she looked at Piers, she saw that his eyes were damp too.

At last Ed stepped back, blew his nose loudly and pulled himself together. 'Now I get to meet Suzy,' he declared, and it was her turn to be gathered up in a bear-hug. 'You don't know the joy it gives me to see you two guys together,' he murmured into her ear, as he released her.

She cast him a puzzled look. The American knew she was accompanying Piers because of her profile—and in the capacity of helpmate—yet his comment had seemed to link them in a personal way. Suzy shrugged. The sentiment of the moment must have confused him.

'Enter, enter,' Ed exhorted, bustling them through a square hallway and into a crowded but comfortably furnished living-room.

As the smell of polish filled her nostrils, Suzy saw that every piece of furniture gleamed, the windows sparkled, the gold on white flowered curtains were freshly washed. Their host and his sons had clearly worked hard and long in preparation for their visit. Coffee and plates of cookies were rapidly provided, and some general chat followed—about their journey, about Piers' injured hand, which he dismissed as his own fault, about how comforted Ed already felt for seeing him.

'I'll show you where you're sleeping,' the American said, when his sons excused themselves and disappeared into a bedroom to watch a favourite TV soap. 'And while you unpack I'll start on dinner. I'm doing chilli con carne—I hope you both like it?' he asked anxiously.

Suzy nodded. 'Very much.'

'And me too,' Piers assured him.

'I've emptied a chest of drawers and half the closet,' Ed said, leading them out through the hallway and along a short corridor. 'There should be sufficient space for your gear, but if not don't hesitate to let me know and——'

Piers placed a calming hand on his shoulder. 'We'll be fine,' he said.

Recognising that he was fussing, the older man smiled. 'The boys are doubling up in Harv's room on the right, and I'm on the left.' He opened a third door and gestured for them to go inside. 'Here we are.'

Decorated in a folksy style, the room contained twin beds with a rough-hewn occasional table set in between. A rough-hewn wardrobe and dressing-table faced each other on opposite walls.

'You have your own facilities,' said Ed, nodding to where a door stood ajar to reveal a small pine-walled bathroom. 'Sorry it's separate beds, but if you want to move them together——' he winked '—I shan't mind.'

Suzy looked at him in bewilderment. She had assumed this to be the first of two rooms which he would be showing them, but it was clear that he expected her and Piers to sleep here together.

'Er—excuse me,' she began.

'We'll be with you when we've unpacked,' Piers cut in, and firmly steered their host back out into the corridor.

'Edmund's put us together!' Suzy protested, the moment the door had closed behind him. 'Why on earth would he do that?' She raised her hand to jab an indignant finger. '*You* told him to!'

CHAPTER SEVEN

PIERS shook his head. 'No.'

'You must have done!'

'Keep your voice down,' he commanded.

'You said you were a seething mass of hormones,' Suzy hissed, 'and——'

'The minute we're alone tonight I'm going to pounce?' Piers interjected, his voice low and trimmed with steel. 'For the past two weeks the only thing separating you and me at night has been unlocked doors, but have I ever walked through them?' His pale grey eyes flickered over her slim figure. 'Have I ever forced you to offer up the delights of your breasts and your thighs to me? Have I ever thrust myself into your body?'

Hot fire scorched her cheeks. There had been times when she had lain awake, wondering if he might be tempted to do just that...and perhaps irrationally and foolishly hoping.

'No,' she admitted, 'but——'

Piers had not finished. 'Though force wouldn't have been necessary,' he rasped. 'Your share of hormones means that should I have chosen to enter your bed you'd have——'

'We were in different rooms at your apartment,' Suzy cut in, determindedly fixing her gaze on a point somewhere beyond his shoulder.

She did not need him to tell her what she would have done. She had a pretty good idea, and the knowledge was not comforting.

'We were also alone where any screams of protest would have gone unheard,' said Piers. 'Whereas here all it would take is one squeak and the Drooling Duo would come galloping in to your rescue.'

'The Drooling Duo?' she queried.

'You must have noticed how Harv and Jason have taken a shine to you. There are two beds,' he went on, and cast the rough-hewn table which sat between them a dry look. 'Plus I'd need to be an Olympic hurdler to get as far as first base.'

'Even so, I refuse to spend the night in here with you,' Suzy said tautly.

Piers lifted a brow. 'You're scared you might feel inspired to try a little hurdling yourself?'

'I am not!' she snapped, her fiery cheeks flaming. 'Keep your voice down!'

'Why would Ed think we wanted to be together?' Suzy asked, returning to her original query. 'Even if you didn't arrange it, you must have said something that gave him the idea.'

Piers walked over to the window. 'I said nothing, but——' he frowned down at the street below '—when we were held hostage I spoke about you.'

'You did?' she said, surprised.

'There was so much time to kill that Ed and I talked about virtually everyone and everything which had happened in our lives,' he said impatiently.

The American's friendliness indicated that Piers' account of her could not have been too damning, but how had he portrayed his role in the events of three

years ago? Suzy wondered. Had he confessed to his
duplicity or, even in the confidences of the hostage
situation, had he shied away from showing himself
up in a bad light?

'What did you say?' she asked.

Piers was dismissive. 'Just that we'd once had a bit
of a thing going. But Ed must have read the wrong
signals and decided that you coming to New York
meant we'd got together again.'

'Whatever he decided, I am *not* sleeping in here
with you!' she declared.

'Tell me again,' said Piers. 'It hasn't quite sunk in.'
His thumbs were hooked into the hip pockets of his
jeans and his long legs placed apart. 'Look, the
prospect of us sharing doesn't have me all a-tingle,
either.'

Suzy said nothing. She was not sure why, but this
declaration made her feel peeved and strangely
deflated.

'However,' he continued, 'as there are only three
bedrooms, you must see that if you insist on going it
alone it'll cause all kinds of trouble.'

'I do, and I'm sorry about that.'

'It pleases Ed to think that we're sweethearts.'

'So I gathered. However, you're going to have to
tell him——'

'I'm telling him nothing,' Piers said flatly. 'You
heard what his sons said about how easily the poor
guy gets upset? If he realised he'd messed up the
sleeping arrangements and that it isn't all Cupids and
pink hearts between us, it'd bother him—and right
now Ed's in too shaky a state to be bothered.'

'I'm supposed to occupy this room with you *and* pretend we're conducting some kind of a—a liaison?' Suzy protested.

'You're not supposed to occupy this room—you will,' he told her. 'And yes, for Ed's sake you'll act as if we're lovers. There's no need to panic—I shan't demand heavy necking, just the occasional affectionate smile will do,' he rasped, when she looked at him askance. 'Now, which bed do you want?'

She did not want either—and whether she would ever be able to sleep with his six feet three inches of fine-honed masculinity stretched out a yard or so away seemed debatable.

'You can have the one nearest to the window,' he said, when she did not reply. 'Hell, it's only for four nights, and it's not as though you're being asked to shack up with a stranger. We do know each other, both on a day-to-day basis and in the Biblical sense,' he said, in a brusque reminder, 'and we have been living cheek-by-jowl in saintly purity for the past two weeks or more. Apart from that night when you came into my room and——'

'The bed nearest the window will be fine,' Suzy declared, taking hold of her suitcase and swinging it on to the bed. 'I'll hang up your shirts and deal with anything else you can't manage,' she offered.

'Thanks.'

As she started to unpack, Suzy felt the foolishness which followed the ebbing of sudden rage. In accusing Piers of fixing the sleeping arrangements, she had jumped to the wrong conclusion. An idiotic conclusion. If he was going to marry the gorgeous—the bandy, her mind added evilly—Amanda Dundas, he would hardly pursue her. She cast him a covert look. She had wondered whether he might break the news to his fellow hostage, but Piers had not even mentioned his girlfriend. Perhaps the marriage was to be kept a strict secret until such time as a Press conference announcement could be arranged? Suzy pulled a face. Knowing Amanda, that seemed probable.

Although they spent an amiable evening chatting with Edmund and his sons, thoughts of bedtime lurked perpetually at the back of Suzy's mind. What she would do, she decided, was undress and change in the bathroom and then, at the speed of light, dart into bed. Once there, she would close her eyes and feign instant sleep. In the morning, the procedure would be reversed. That way, her awareness of her roommate and any contact with him would be kept to a minimum.

As it turned out, her planning was unnecessary. At eleven o'clock when she started to yawn, Piers and their host were earnestly reminiscing. Suzy said goodnight and left them to it. After showering, she returned to the bedroom to find herself still alone and, with relief, slid between the sheets. A victim of a late night the previous night and the day's travel, she fell asleep as soon as her head touched the pillow. What time Piers came to bed she did not know, but when she awoke the next morning he was deep asleep.

Shifting on to her side, Suzy gazed across the gap between their two beds. Piers lay on his stomach, with his face half turned into the pillow and one bare arm hanging down to the floor. His dark hair was tousled and the faint shadow of beard growth darkened his jaw. She heaved a sigh. Even asleep, he possessed a compelling male magnetism.

'How about us taking in Central Park this morning?' Harv suggested eagerly, when she joined him and his brother in the kitchen for breakfast.

Edmund was still recovering from extreme exhaustion and so, he had explained with profuse apologies the previous evening, would not be around to do duty as a morning host.

'I'd like that,' Suzy agreed.

'We could go for a ride in one of the horse-drawn carriages,' said Jason, adjusting the Stars and Stripes headband which had replaced his baseball cap.

Throughout the meal Suzy kept waiting for Piers to appear, but he didn't; and when she crept back into the bedroom he was still asleep. Quietly collecting up her gear, she departed without disturbing him.

The trip to Central Park was fun—Harv and Jason made it fun. Apparently deciding that competing for her attention was pointless, they joined forces to become a carefree admiring pair. Each had a store of atrociously corny one-liners which kept Suzy laughing and such an open all-American manner that she soon felt as if she had known them for ever.

On their return to the apartment, they discovered that the two ex-hostages had also enjoyed their day. After a long, easy, relaxed chat, Piers had coaxed the photographer out of doors for his first walk since their release.

Intent on re-employing her avoidance technique, that evening Suzy waited until the two men were, once again, deep in conversation and then took her leave. However, this time when she came out of the bathroom she found Piers stretched out full-length on his bed, hands linked behind his head. Her heart bumped. His shirt, which was unbuttoned and pulled loose from his trousers, had fallen down to reveal a tanned chest covered in whorls of crisp dark hair.

Marching between the two beds, she briskly drew back her covers. 'Goodnight.'

'What on earth are you wearing?' demanded Piers, sitting up and swinging his feet to the floor.

Suzy tugged at her oversized white T-shirt. 'It's the fashion. Lots of women sleep in them,' she informed him airily.

'Not women who pack a nightdress in their suitcase,' he retorted.

She flushed. She had not reckoned on him being so sharp-eyed. But her nightdress was the shoestring-strapped, low-bodiced confection she had worn on the night when she had entered his room.

'I was cold,' she declared.

'Cold, in a temperature of what must be close on eighty degrees?' Piers rose to his feet. 'What are you wearing underneath it?'

'That's none of your business,' Suzy said primly.

'So to find out, I'm going to have to take hold of the hem and pull the T-shirt up until it's around your neck?' he enquired.

The smile which lurked in the corner of his mouth said Piers was teasing, and yet, standing close to her in the confined space, he seemed very tall, very male, very dangerous.

'I'm wearing bikini briefs,' she gabbled, flustered by his threat.

'But no bra.'

'No,' she agreed.

His eyes dipped to where the dark stains of her nipples were visible beneath the white cotton and, as if in response, she felt her breasts pucker and tighten.

'That was a statement, not a question,' drawled Piers. 'You don't need to tell me, because I can see for myself.'

Furious with him for arousing her, and with herself for becoming aroused, Suzy starfished a hand on his chest.

'Excuse me!' she said, and thrust him out of the way.

As Piers dropped back on to his bed, she clambered into hers and yanked the sheet up beneath her chin. Even if she was in danger of heat-stroke, she would continue to wear the T-shirt—though now she wished it had been thicker. Much thicker. Abruptly, Suzy raised her head. She had not seen what her roommate had worn to bed the previous night, but now...

'You're not intending to sleep in the—the nude?' she asked.

Piers shrugged. 'It's my usual practice,' he said, his voice casual and maddeningly calm.

Suzy's heart began to pound. 'But it wouldn't be...not with....I'm here,' she faltered.

He chuckled. 'I thought I might need to go back and forth to a bathroom, so I've brought pyjamas. Though only the trousers.'

She gave a limp smile. This time she did not say goodnight. She did not say anything. She just lay back on the pillow and shut her eyes. Tight.

The following evening, when Suzy went to change for dinner, Piers followed her into the bedroom.

'I'll have a shower after you,' he said, and, stripping off his shirt, he lounged beside the open window.

As she took her jumpsuit from the wardrobe, she tried not to look at him, but her eyes were drawn; to the gleam of his skin, to the flat brown discs of his nipples, to the jeans which emphasised the muscles of his thighs and left his masculinity in no doubt. Clutching the jumpsuit to her, Suzy strode into the bathroom. Piers attracted her, distracted her, had got under her skin. But in just two more days they would be on their way home, she consoled herself. And the day after that, she would be going to live alone and blessedly unharassed.

'All yours,' she announced, when she emerged ten minutes later.

As Piers went off to shower, she sat down at the dressing-table and started to make up her face. It would not take long, and she intended to be finished and gone before he reappeared. A shimmer of taupe colour had been applied to her eyelids, and she was brushing her lashes with mascara, when the bathroom door opened. Glancing round, she saw Piers with a towel knotted around his hips and another held in his hand. Her pulses tripped. She stiffened. The last time she had seen him clad in a towel, he had removed it.

'Could you dry my back for me?' he asked. 'It's not so easy with one hand.'

'You've managed before,' Suzy protested, her agitation adding a tartness to her tone.

'Only just, and you were never so available before.'

To refuse would have been petty, so she rose and took the towel. 'How did things go with Ed today?' she enquired, as she began to rub.

Conversation seemed essential, if she was to escape being swamped by the awareness of what she was doing.

Piers looked at her over his shoulder. 'Being able to track back over what happened to us appears to be helping, and this time it was he who suggested that we went for a walk.'

'Did anyone recognise you?'

He nodded. 'There were several waves of acknowledgment and a couple of people came up to commiserate. I wondered if it'd throw Ed, but he was OK.' Piers lifted a brow. 'And how was your sightseeing with the Drooling Duo?'

'Great.' Suzy had dried the bronzed length of his back, from the width of his shoulders down to the narrowness of his waist. 'Finished,' she announced thankfully.

To Suzy's dismay, Piers' appearance in the towel proved to be the forerunner of him spending an interminable time in a state of undress. At bedtime and the next morning, when he awoke within minutes of her, he wandered around half naked for what seemed like hours. She realised she was being over-sensitive and told herself to ignore him, but her senses were agonisingly aware. Suzy also told herself that now— alleluia!—they had reached the last whole day of their stay.

'What do you have lined up for this morning?' Piers enquired, as he sat with her and the boys at the breakfast table.

'The helicopter trip,' said Harv.

'Decided to save the best for the last,' Jason explained, and grinned at Suzy. 'I might train to be a helicopter pilot,' he declared, with youthful bravado. 'Buzzing around in the air all the time, rescuing people from oil rigs and burning buildings. Wow!'

'If you don't mind, I'd like to join you,' said Piers.

Harv smiled. 'Please do.'

Suzy's heart knotted. The teenager might not mind, but she did. She had been banking on another day without Piers. Banking on having time apart, in which she could shore up what was becoming an increasingly precarious composure.

'Is Pop accompanying us as well?' Jason asked.

Piers shook his head. 'I've persuaded him to have an extra long lie-in and take the day slow and easy.'

'Good idea,' said Suzy, as she buttered a blueberry muffin. Edmund was trying so hard to be the hospitable host, and she had been worried about him overdoing things. In particular, while he had smilingly rejected all her offers of help, it was obvious that he found the production of the evening meal something of a strain. 'Why don't we leave him a note saying we'll bring in a take-away this evening?' she suggested.

'No need,' said Piers. 'We're going out to dinner.'

'Dad's happy to do that?' Harv protested.

'It was his idea. Apparently there's a French restaurant a few blocks away which has private rooms——'

'The food there is five-star,' Harv inserted.

'——and he's booked one.' Piers grinned. 'He's also told the *maître d'* to put the champagne on ice.'

'Ace!' Jason exclaimed.

Piers reached across the table and took hold of Suzy's hand. 'It'll be ace to spend a day with my girl,' he murmured.

She shot him a wary glance. This far, they had only been together in the evenings and then were part of a group and caught up in conversation. There had been no necessity, and little opportunity, to act the part of lovers. But his statement and his handclasp warned that the situation was about to change.

The helicopters flew from a concrete dock alongside the East River. Tickets bought, they joined a queue of other tourists, and as they waited helicopters of various sizes whirlygigged down, deposited and collected passengers, and whirlygigged off again. In time, their number was called and they were led out beneath noisily spinning blades to a tiny four-seater. Suzy sat facing the front with Piers beside her, while Harv and Jason were opposite. Behind them, concealed by a partition, was the pilot.

As the door clanged shut, she frowned. 'I think it's odd not being able to see the pilot,' she said, speaking in a low voice. 'I mean, suppose he had a heart attack and we didn't know?'

'There'll be a law which insists he has frequent health checks,' Piers told her.

A moment later, the helicopter rose from the concrete pad. It juddered, tilted at a breath-catching angle and set off up into the sky. As Suzy watched the ground fall further and further away beneath them, she sat rigid. Goosebumps chilled her skin. To soar like a bird and have a bird's eye view was magical, yet she wished she had never come. Flying across the Atlantic had not caused her one moment of worry, but the helicopter seemed so flimsy, so at the whim of the elements. And it was possible to be given the all-clear by a doctor one day, and still be felled by a coronary the next.

She was telling herself not to be such a scare-monger—and such a coward—when Piers covered her hand with his.

'There's no need to be frightened,' he said, speaking below the battering sound of the machine so that Harv and Jason could not hear. 'I've toured war zones in these things for years, and they've always been reliable.'

'Could you fly one?' Suzy demanded.

'I reckon so, at a pinch.' He squeezed her hand and smiled. 'But it won't come to that, I promise.'

Soon they were high above the tallest of the sky-scrapers and looking down on their roofs. Some carried air-conditioning machinery, some were planted with gardens, others had glass domes which glittered and sparkled in the sun.

'Isn't it fantastic?' Harv yelled.

'The thrill of a lifetime,' Jason proclaimed.

'Beats anything I've ever seen before,' said Piers.

Suzy smiled brightly. 'It's wonderful!'

It was wonderful, and she knew her fear was fool-ishness, but as they crossed Manhattan Island and went out over the water, she clung on tight to Piers' hand.

'Only a few more minutes now,' he whispered, as their teenage companions excitedly pointed out landmarks.

'I know,' she said, but although her voice did not squeak, it would have won no prizes for resonance.

Piers put his arm around her.

With the blue of the sky above them and the water blue below, they flew out to the huge figure of the Statue of Liberty. After circling it for an awesome panoramic view, the helicopter headed back over the island and not much later, they landed.

As soon as she stepped back on to solid ground, Suzy felt better—yet when Piers kept his arm around her, she did not pull away. If he wanted them to act like lovers, why not? They were a long way from home, with people she would never meet again, so today could be—would be, she decided—regarded as a time out of time. A time when, instead of resisting, she would relax and go along with him.

Next their teenage escorts took them to a stylish shopping mall where Suzy bought postcards and gifts for her parents, and then they had lunch in the mall's glass-roofed brasserie. Later they explored Chinatown and finished the afternoon with a visit to an art museum. Throughout the day, Piers reached for her hand, held her close, gazed fondly into her eyes—and throughout the day Suzy responded. She knew they were involved in a conscious demonstration of togetherness for Harv and Jason's benefit, yet it all seemed so natural...and was very seductive.

Her behaviour could be accused of being less than circumspect, she reflected, as she undressed in the bathroom that evening. It could be said to have been foolhardy. She shrugged. She was not going to worry about it now, not when the champagne continued to add a zing to her blood and she still floated on the evening's good-humoured air.

Her teeth cleaned and her T-shirt donned, Suzy sauntered back into the bedroom. Her footsteps faltered. Once again she had done her disappearing trick and left Piers enjoying a nightcap with their host, but now he was sitting on his bed with his back towards her, one-handedly removing his shoes and socks. His shirt had been thrown on to a chair and, as he bent, her gaze moved across the breadth of his shoulders and down the long golden length of his back. Her palms began to tingle. She could imagine running her hands down his back, feeling the warmth of his skin beneath her fingertips.

'You'd like to stroke me?' Piers enquired.

Suzy blinked, startled to find him so accurately reading her mind, but then her eyes met his in the dressing-table mirror. Hot circles of pink bloomed on her cheeks. He had been watching her, watching him.

'The bathroom's clear,' she said.

Rising, he turned to face her. 'You want me out of your sight? Why? Could it be that my naked torso has you aching with lust? Are you longing to rip away my clothes and do all kinds of unspeakable things to me?'

She looked at him and, all of a sudden, everything dropped into place.

'You've been doing it on purpose!' she exclaimed.

'Doing what?' asked Piers. 'And there's no need to tell the entire household.'

'Standing around half-clothed like—like a male stripper!' she hissed.

She knew she should be indignant, if not furious, yet instead she felt amused and absurdly pleased.

'Would I do something so diabolical?' he said.

Stepping forward, she grabbed a handful of the hair on his chest and gave it a tweak. 'Yes, you would!'

Her reprimand complete, she was turning away when Piers suddenly shot out an arm and half lifted, half propelled her down on to her bed. Before there was time to protest, she was flat on her back with him straddling her.

'That hurt!' he complained, rubbing vigorously at his chest.

Suzy gazed up. 'Hard luck, mister. It was meant to.'

The corner of his mouth dimpled. 'But you've enjoyed ogling me.'

'I did *not* ogle,' she declared, as haughty as a duchess.

'You ogled morning, noon and night,' Piers asserted, and started tickling her.

Suzy giggled, she squirmed, she did her best to push him away. But even with one hand out of action, her assailant easily overpowered her.

'I may have . . . noticed you . . . from time to time,' she conceded, gasping out the words between fits of laughter, 'but anyone would . . . find it difficult not to. . . . notice the Incredible Hulk.'

Piers clutched hold of the front of her T-shirt in a large fist and yanked her up off the bed and against him.

'Incredible Hulk?' he demanded, in mock outrage.

'Do you have to hold me quite so close?' Suzy enquired.

She pulled back, but he refused to let go. She twisted. She turned. Rip! There was a tearing sound, and when she looked down she saw that the side seams on her T-shirt had given way and now a large hole gaped beneath each arm.

'Thanks!' she protested.

Piers stared at the rounded sideswell of her breasts which had been exposed. 'It's a big improvement.'

As his eyes lifted to hers, the air between them seemed to shimmer with energy. The mood had changed. They were no longer fooling around.

'You think so?' Suzy said quietly.

'I'm certain,' Piers replied and, letting her down on to the bed, he lowered his dark head and kissed the side of one silky cream-skinned breast.

'That feels nice,' she murmured.

'How about this?' he asked, pressing his mouth to the other breast.

'Nice, too.'

He lay down beside her. 'And now?' he enquired, and kissed her lips.

Suzy never got to give a verdict, for all of a sudden they were kissing feverishly, fervently, locked mouth to mouth and unable to pull away. Then legs were wrapped around legs and Piers was half on top of her, and the T-shirt had been twisted aside and his hands were covering her breasts and he was pinching her nipples and she was making little animal sounds and——

Outside in the street, a police siren wailed.

'What are we doing?' Suzy demanded, jerking back to stare at Piers in consternation.

His eyes smiled. 'I'd call it foreplay.'

'We can't!'

Desire was said to have no reason, but she had taken leave of her senses—total leave. However seductive it might have been, Piers' fondness towards her was a pretence, a sham. And as for today being a time out of time and not mattering—it was a nice theory, but... Had he played the lover with the deliberate idea of softening her up? Suzy wondered. Did he intend her to be his last fling before he married? A sob of anguish rose up in her throat. She knew from bitter experience that he was a man with no scruples, no heart, yet she had allowed him to bewitch her. Again.

'Suzy, we must,' said Piers, in a husky driven voice. He placed a muscled arm around her, imprisoning her with his strength. 'These last few days have been hell. Sleeping beside you, wanting you. Having you so near and yet——'

'No!' she insisted.

He drew in harsh controlling breaths. 'Have you taken a vow of chastity?' he demanded, managing to sound savage and sarcastic and joky, all at the same time.

Suzy pulled the T-shirt over her. 'I've—I've just changed my mind.'

'God almighty!' Piers scythed, but he released her. As she scrambled from the bed, he sat up. 'What are you trying to do to me?' he demanded, running a hand violently through his hair as though he wanted to tear it out by the roots. 'I'm not made of stone!'

Guilt began to gnaw. She ought never to have allowed things to go so far—and she wouldn't have done if he had not bewitched her, and if she had not been drinking champagne.

'I'm sorry I'm not fulfilling your expectations,' she said, frowning, 'but——'

'You thought you'd try and push me to the limit?' Piers' lips drew back from his teeth in a tight smile. 'Congratulations, you've damn near succeeded.'

A flush ran up her fine-boned face. A man with less self-discipline—probably most men—would have ignored her protests and made her submit.

'There's a name for women like you,' he went on angrily. 'Women who—— Oh, what the hell,' he snarled, and strode away into the bathroom.

When he emerged, he snapped a curt goodnight and switched off the light. Lying in her bed, Suzy wondered whether the emotional charge of their argument would keep him awake. It did, for half an hour, but then the rhythm of his breathing told her he had gone to sleep. Looking across at him in the faint golden light from the street lamps, she felt an ache behind her ribcage. Now she wished they had made love. Should she creep across into his bed? she wondered. She wanted to. She wanted to share Piers' bed and, she realised, in a moment of startling clarity, she wanted to share the rest of her life with him. The ache behind her ribs changed into a violent hammering of her heart. She loved him.

Twisting on to her back, she stared desolately at the ceiling. She had been so sure she had laid their relationship to rest and worked Piers Armstrong out of her system, but she had been deceiving herself. All she had done was bury her feelings deep inside her where, for three years, they had lain like a sleeping volcano waiting to erupt. It did not matter that all she had ever been to him was a naïve young playmate who had boosted his masculine ego. However he had treated her, she had continued to love him. She had never stopped. As the guerrilla group had once held him captive, so Piers continued to hold her captive— a prisoner of love.

Suzy bit deep into her lip. Why else had she gone to see his father when he had disappeared? She might have wanted to comfort Hugo, but she had also needed to establish some link—no matter how tenuous—with his missing son. Why else had she offered to help with Piers' campaign? Why else had she reacted so violently when Randolph Gardener had said he wanted him to be included in her book? And why else did she feel such a bitter and unusually bitchy dislike for Amanda Dundas?

Suzy punched at her pillow. But Piers had not cared about her three years ago, and he did not now. He might want to make love to her, but the attraction was physical. Just physical. He had never, ever, said he loved her. She frowned. His wish to make love could even be fuelled by revenge. Piers believed that she had slept with him for a purpose, so he could have decided to retaliate by cold-bloodedly seducing her. Suzy's insides hollowed. She did not think so, but then she did not want to think so.

If only she had followed her instincts when Randolph Gardener had mentioned his name and refused to have anything to do with him, she thought wretchedly. If only they had stuck to that purely practical working relationship. Suzy turned on to her side, away from Piers. It was too late for 'if onlys'—though she refused to spend the rest of her life in thrall. What she would do was leave his apartment, finish the profile, and then forget about him. She really would. Her eyes were closed. So roll on tomorrow and going home.

'Would you care for a newspaper?' the cabin steward asked, smiling at Suzy. He brandished the selection he carried. 'We have today's editions of both American and English ones.'

She scanned the titles and chose a New York journal.

The steward's smile switched.

'And you, sir?'

'I'd like a copy of *The View*, please,' said Piers.

After glancing at the headlines, Suzy tucked the paper away in the seat pocket in front of her. She would take another look once they were airborne.

'Do I assume from Ed's recital of the questions he was asked and the answers he gave that he sailed through the Press conference?' she enquired.

That afternoon, while she had gone with Harv and Jason for a walk around SoHo, Piers and his fellow hostage had faced the media at a Broadway hotel. An impressively large number of reporters and TV crews had turned up, and the meeting had lasted longer than expected. The two men were barely back at the apartment before it was time to pile into the Buick and head for the airport. Ed, who had insisted on coming to see them off, had talked non-stop all the way.

'He did,' said Piers, and cast her a wry glance. 'So you needn't have worried.'

'I thought he might have found the experience stressful and broken down.'

'And you spent the afternoon on pins?'

'More or less,' she confessed, 'but your visit has obviously worked wonders. How about you,' Suzy went on, 'did you find the Press conference hard going?'

'I can't say I enjoyed being in the limelight again, but I've answered similar questions many times before, so it wasn't too much of a strain.' Piers stretched his arms above his head. 'Just a bit tiring.'

She looked around. Apart from a couple sitting two rows ahead of them and a trio of solitary businessmen, the first class cabin was empty.

'It's peaceful in here,' she said, 'so we should be able to get some sleep tonight.'

'And you need to sleep, if you're to be bright-eyed and bushy-tailed ready for moving into your new place the day after tomorrow,' he observed.

'True,' Suzy agreed, with a smile, but as the plane taxied along the runway her smile faded.

Piers had sounded as though he couldn't wait to get rid of her, but his frustration last night and his continued hostility today were an over-reaction. Amanda Dundas's body language had made it plain that, ever since his release, all he had needed to do was snap his fingers and she would hop into bed. It wasn't as though he had been living like a monk!

When they were heading out east over the ocean, the young steward reappeared to distribute dinner menus.

'I'll be back to take your orders,' he said, 'but while you're deciding perhaps you'd care for a drink?'

'Sparkling mineral water for me, please,' said Suzy.

'And I'll have a gin and tonic,' Piers told him. 'There was one question at the Press conference which threw me,' he said, when their drinks had been placed on the arm table between them. 'Someone raised a query about Amanda——' he paused '—and the engagement.'

Engagement? The word sliced to a nerve, and Suzy flinched. So she had it at last, confirmation that Piers was to marry the actress. He *can't*! she thought, all her previous protests firing up again. However he had treated her, he didn't deserve such a fate. She would put him wise about Amanda, she decided. She must. But what could she say without appearing mean-spirited or it sounding as if it was sour grapes? Her brow crimped. And wasn't there an element of sour grapes involved? Wouldn't she be warning him off because it hurt—it *crucified* her—to think of Piers married to someone else? Suzy drank from her glass. Even if her motives were mixed, she still felt compelled to speak.

'You hadn't expected Amanda to make the announcement during your absence?' she said, wondering how best to approach the subject. Though whether she did so obliquely or head-on, she was still in the business of condemning his bride.

'No. But how come you seem to know about it?' Piers asked curiously. 'The man who asked for my comments said the report had only just appeared in the UK Press.'

'I just—well, I guessed,' she said awkwardly, and took a breath. 'You aren't going to like this, but I feel it's my duty to——'

'So tell me, what's this fellow, Wally Seabrook, got to offer?' he interrupted.

Confused, Suzy looked at him. The only Wally Seabrook she could think of was a millionaire building contractor whose activities were occasionally reported in the papers, but what did he have do with anything?

'Wally Seabrook?' she repeated.

'Amanda's fiancé.'

'Her fiancé?' she echoed, in bewilderment.

'Who did you think she was marrying?' Piers asked.

Suzy moistened her lips. 'Um . . . you.'

CHAPTER EIGHT

'ME? Me marry Amanda Dundas?' Piers gave a hoot of derisive laughter. 'Credit me with having at least half a brain!' Taking hold of his newspaper, he started to leaf through. 'Maybe the engagement's mentioned in here.'

'There it is,' said Suzy, as he reached the what's-happening-around-town column.

When she pointed at a photograph of Amanda Dundas, smiling a dazzling smile and arm in arm with a portly, bulbous-nosed, elderly man, Piers stared.

'That's Wally Seabrook?' he said incredulously.

'It is.'

'When she told me about "her friend"——' he placed the phrase between pithy inverted commas '—Amanda neglected to mention that he was a senior citizen.' He read the item. 'Or that he was rolling in bucks. But now I know what he has to offer.'

'They're tying the knot next month,' Suzy said, her eyes skimming over the report. 'That's quick.'

'Yes, though you can be sure Amanda will have given it a great deal of shrewd, calculating consideration,' he said disparagingly. 'However, despite the guy's wealth, I'm surprised she hasn't gone for someone who could have been of advantage in her career.'

'She has. He can. Twice over the past year, Wally Seabrook has used some of his substantial wealth to

167

back shows,' Suzy explained. 'He's been quoted as saying he doesn't know anything about show-business, but he finds it fascinating.'

'Another fact which Amanda neglected to mention,' Piers remarked. 'And, as a backer, old Wally would seem to be ideally placed to suggest that his bride be given a part—a big one—in any future shows.'

'Have you decided what you'd like for dinner?' asked the steward, coming up to smile at Suzy.

She took a belated look at the menu. 'Grapefruit cocktail, chicken in tarragon sauce, and raspberry pavlova,' she said.

'And the same for me,' Piers told him.

'Something to drink with the meal, sir?'

He checked the wine list. 'As I recall, you like Chardonnay,' he said to Suzy. She nodded. 'We'll have a bottle of the '89, please. Amanda may regard marrying Seabrook as a smart career move,' Piers remarked, when they were alone again, 'but it could turn out to be just as unproductive as attaching herself to me has been. After all, one role in a TV sit-com is nothing to get excited about. You said you felt it your duty to...what?' he asked, taking an abrupt leap back in the conversation.

Suzy gave a rueful smile. 'I was going to tell you how Amanda had used your campaign for self-promotion, but you obviously already know.'

'I've known for a long time.' Piers took a mouthful of gin and tonic. 'I'd better explain.'

'Please.'

'I've wanted to explain ever since she told me about Wally Seabrook——'

'That was on the night of Hugo's party?' Suzy cut in.

'Yes. But she could have been lying about her friendship with him, as she lied about her friendship with me, so it seemed wiser to wait until I knew for certain that I'd got her off my back.' Piers tapped the newspaper and grinned. 'Now I do.'

'Amanda lied about her friendship with you?' Suzy queried.

He nodded. 'When she approached my father about speaking in my campaign, she told him we'd had something heavy going. However, for eight or nine months before I was kidnapped we'd never even set eyes on each other, and prior to that, although we had met, it was only from time to time.' He sighed. 'However, our lack of contact meant that Hugo had no idea what was, or wasn't, happening in my private life, so he believed her.'

'You didn't strike me as being enraptured with Amanda, but I was fooled too,' said Suzy. 'And Randolph Gardener reckons I'm perceptive!'

'If my father had accepted the woman as my girl-friend, then it followed that everyone else would,' Piers protested, 'and there was no reason for you to question it.'

'I suppose not.'

'Though she isn't my type.' He grimaced. 'Too ar-tificial, too self-centred.'

'You said the two of you had met, from time to time,' Suzy reminded him.

'Yes, though it was always at Amanda's suggestion.'

'Why go, if you didn't particularly like her?'

Piers examined the contents of his glass. 'Because after you and I broke up I felt . . . at a loose end.'

'You went out with Amanda *after* we split?' she enquired, frowning.

'Yes. Whenever I arrived back from an assignment she seemed to ring suggesting a drink or dinner, and I'd think that going out might cheer me up, but it never did. However, although it took a while—at that point all I could think about was you—it gradually penetrated that Amanda was only pursuing me because I was my father's son. From then on, I stopped seeing her.'

'She must have fancied you too,' Suzy protested. 'I mean, you're——' On the brink of launching into a glowing giveway description, she stopped dead. 'Amanda must have fancied you,' she insisted.

'Maybe a bit,' Piers said curtly, 'but she fancied the help she hoped Hugo would provide if we teamed up even more.'

'Hugo may have been another reason for her becoming involved in your campaign,' Suzy mused. 'Amanda could have thought he'd be so full of gratitude that he'd drop her name in all the right ears.'

'I'm sure she did. However, to quote my father, "because her talent is such that she's a far better advertisement for her aerobics class than her acting school", he maintained a discreet silence.'

'Amanda might be a dead loss on stage, yet she acted your girlfriend to perfection,' Suzy remarked wryly.

'Didn't she just!' Piers drained his glass. 'But to find myself claimed by a woman who was universally perceived as my self-sacrificing and ever-loving soulmate put me in a hell of a fix. On the one hand, I deeply resented the fact that she'd been milking my being held hostage for all it was worth——'

'How quickly did you realise?'

'I had my suspicions from the start, but a few discreet questions asked around confirmed it within days. Amanda's sharp practice is why, when we met at the clinic, I accused you of being an opportunist,' he continued. 'It had made me wary of everyone else, so when you waltzed in and talked about including me in your book, it seemed as if you were also hoping to cash in on my misfortune.' Piers ran his index finger along the back of her wrist. 'I'm sorry.'

Suzy smiled. 'It was understandable.'

'However, on the other hand,' he said, picking up the thread he had left hanging, 'I was afraid that if I gave the woman the cold shoulder she'd kick up a public fuss. She could have portrayed herself as the cruelly rejected girlfriend and sold her story to the tabloids.'

'You can count on it. To a publicity freak like Amanda, any kind is better than none.'

'I was damned if I'd give her the pleasure,' Piers said grittily, 'so all I could do was wait for my celebrity status to dwindle, make it clear I offered nothing more publicity-wise, and pray she'd lose interest.'

'Which is why you wouldn't go out with her,' Suzy said. 'There was no claustrophobia.'

He grinned. 'None. Though you never believed there was.'

'Dinnertime,' announced the steward, arriving to fix table-trays in front of them.

The trays were covered in white damask cloths and laid with sparkling glasses and gleaming silver. With much finesse and smiling attention, the meal was served.

'How did Amanda explain the pretence of being your girlfriend to you?' asked Suzy, when they had finished their main course and were awaiting the arrival of dessert.

'She didn't. From meeting me at the airport— something which I found completely bewildering—she acted as though we'd been close. For the first couple of days I was too busy acclimatising to question it, but when I did she claimed that what we'd had previously had been special.' Piers snorted. 'She was talking gibberish and she knew it! I told her she was mistaken, and from then on did my best to keep her at arm's length——' he rolled his eyes '—which was difficult, and make it plain that I wouldn't be inveigled into a relationship. Though I had to do it without arousing anyone else's suspicions and without upsetting her.'

'But Amanda felt there was still some mileage to be gained from you.'

Piers grimaced. 'Apparently. I'd hoped that by the time I left the clinic she'd be easing off, yet still the damn woman came on strong! I had visions of her suggesting she move in with me, but——' his lips curved '—I forestalled her by getting you to move in instead.'

'That's why you wanted me there? And I thought it was because you needed my support!' Suzy said indignantly.

'I did, that was a consideration too.'

She gave him an old-fashioned look. 'Oh yes?'

'Cross my heart and hope to die,' Piers declared. 'I liked—I like—having you around.'

Suzy refused to be beguiled. 'Amanda didn't like me being around,' she said.

'No, though she didn't complain too excessively, which makes me think she probably had her hooks embedded in Wally Seabrook before I was released. And the speed of their engagement makes it look that way.'

'What did you say at the party which persuaded Amanda to transfer her interest?' Suzy asked, intrigued.

'I told her that being there that evening had made me realise just how unready I was to mix and what a long time it would be before I risked going out again. Months.'

'Months?' she protested.

'I laid it on thick and was full of earnest apologies about how my need to stay home would continue to cramp her style.' Piers grinned. 'Next thing I know, she's revealing how she has this friend who's sweet on her, and, to be fair to me and to him, she thinks we ought to call it a day.'

'Which is why you were so euphoric.'

'In seventh heaven.'

Suzy tilted her head. 'Is Amanda the reason why you want to take a look at my finished manuscript?' she asked.

Piers nodded. 'I felt she might persuade you to write something about her, but I'm determined that, so far as is possible, I'll stop the woman squeezing another ounce of publicity out of me.'

'I haven't written about her,' she told him.

'I didn't think you had, and thanks. When the reporter asked me about Amanda's engagement, I deliberately kept my comments to the minimum,' Piers went on. 'I said we'd only ever been friends and that I hoped she and Mr Seabrook would be happy.'

'Dessert,' the steward announced.

As she ate the cream-laden and calorific meringue, Suzy's head buzzed. She seemed to be suffering from an overload of information, for, although she now knew she had got a lot of things wrong, she was not sure how many.

'Since we met again, if something untoward happens you seem to jump to the automatic conclusion that I must be up to no good,' Piers remarked, when they were drinking cups of rich dark coffee. 'Why? What have I ever done to deserve such a reaction?'

'I'm beginning to think that you didn't do very much,' Suzy said regretfully. 'You see, long before Amanda lied to your father about your relationship, she lied about it to me.'

He looked baffled. 'To you? But when?'

'Do you remember the day, three years ago, after we'd——' She hesitated, and started again. 'Do you remember the day after the awards dinner, how you went off to Peru?'

'I remember.' His eyes met hers, their irises pale grey, the pupils velvet-black. 'I remember everything about that time.'

'Well, while you were away I was sent to interview Amanda for the women's page, and afterwards she asked me if I knew the girl you were involved with at *The View*.'

Piers frowned. 'Why would she do that?'

'Then I had no idea, but now I'd say she'd decided to make a play for you and wanted to check out the opposition. I wondered whether she might recognise me and remember us meeting when she saw me at your apartment,' Suzy recalled, 'but she didn't seem to.'

'She wouldn't. The only person Amanda would ever remember in a situation is herself,' he said drily. 'Did you tell her the girl was you?'

'No, though I blushed so much that I'm sure she realised.'

'Why didn't you tell her?'

'Because she'd already given me the impression that the two of you were ... lovers.'

'We weren't,' Piers objected harshly. 'I've never slept with the woman.'

Suzy gave a strained smile. 'I realise that now.' And I realise why you were so frustrated last night, she thought silently.

'But you thought we were lovers?' he prompted.

She lowered her head. 'I'm afraid so,' she said unhappily. 'In retrospect, I think I'd always felt slightly out of my depth with you, a little in awe of your sophistication, and so for you to be simultaneously involved with a slick-chick actress didn't seem too farfetched.'

'Do you feel out of your depth and in awe now?' Piers enquired.

Her head shot up. 'No way!'

He grinned. 'I didn't think you did.'

'But also,' Suzy said, gravely continuing her tale, 'Amanda said you'd been with her on the day you left for Peru—though you'd told me you were leaving in the morning, and——'

'I was supposed to, but I didn't,' he cut in. 'When I arrived home the airline rang to let me know that the flight had been severely delayed and passengers were not to check in until the afternoon, so I decided to go and see my father. I hadn't seen him for ages. When I arrived I found him providing brunch for a gang of fellow actors, and amongst them was Amanda. I seem to remember that she'd wangled her way in as a friend of a friend.' He took a mouthful of coffee. 'What did she say which made you think we were lovers?'

'She talked about how you'd had a get-together that day.'

'We both happened to be at Hugo's, that was all,' Piers said. 'She cornered me and we exchanged a few words, but they were brief.'

'Amanda made it sound as though it had just been the two of you,' Suzy told him. 'In bed. She said she'd seen your bruised shoulder, and for her to see it you must have taken off your shirt and so, as she was implying intimacy, I thought——'

'She didn't see my shoulder.'

'Then how did she know about it?'

'I'm not sure.' Piers rubbed at his jaw, thinking back. 'I was speaking to Barbara in the kitchen,' he started slowly, 'and while we were talking my father came in and gave me one of his hearty pats on the back. It hurt, and when I complained, Hugo demanded to know why. I explained, and he commiserated.' Piers stopped. 'Yes, that's what must have happened. His voice carries, and Amanda must have been coming to the kitchen to freshen up her drink and overheard.' He shot her a frowning glance. 'I'd been speaking to Barbara about you, and after Hugo went away I continued. Amanda must have hung around and overheard that too.'

'You were telling Barbara how I'd thrown myself at you?' Suzy enquired, her voice sharpening as the old raw feelings of humiliation returned. 'How I was pathetically starry-eyed? How laughable I was?'

'Is that what Amanda said?' he demanded.

'Yes, though she reckoned it was the two of you who'd spoken about me in that way. On the night of the awards dinner I know I threw myself at you, but I was young and——' to her dismay, Suzy heard her voice crack and suddenly she found she was fighting back the tears '—and I cared for you.'

Piers stared at her. 'Oh, God,' he said, 'and that's why you claimed that our night together hadn't meant anything and all you'd wanted was to get rid of your virginity?'

'I needed to salvage some kind of pride,' she mumbled.

'But I thought——'

'More coffee?' the steward enquired, holding out the pot.

They both shook their heads.

'It's true that I did tell Barbara how, after weeks of me holding back, you'd finally brought matters to a head by coaxing me into bed,' Piers said, when the man had retreated. 'That was one reason why I went round to my father's—I desperately needed to talk to someone about it, about us, and I knew Barbara would listen. But I swear I never mocked you. I wouldn't. For me the situation was serious. Suzy, I was in love with you.'

Her mind seemed to unravel. 'In—in love with me?' she faltered.

'Yes, only I didn't know what to do about it.' Piers sighed. 'Until I met you, I'd dated girls who were pleasant company, good fun, but who weren't interested in settling down,' he explained. 'Which suited me fine, because settling down didn't appeal to me either. You see, I wasn't sure whether I had what it took to sustain a long-term relationship, and I happen to believe that marriage is for keeps.'

'What made you think you were unable to sustain a relationship?' asked Suzy.

'My father,' he said simply.

'You're not like him,' she protested.

'In some ways I am. From time to time I catch myself saying something and I think, oh hell, that sounds just like Hugo. And in the years since my mother died, he'd moved from one woman to the next—never caring too much, always losing interest.'

'Perhaps he was searching for someone to replace her?'

'And in Barbara he's found her? Could be,' Piers mused. 'Barbara reminds me of my mother. However,' he went on, 'at that time it seemed it could be my destiny to follow my father's example. But when I was held hostage I undertook some rational self-analysis and I realised that I am *me*——' he prodded a thumb in his chest '—not him.'

'Good,' Suzy said, and cast him a look. 'You thought I wanted to settle down?'

'I was sure of it. Don't misunderstand me, I'm not saying marriage was a conscious goal to be achieved within the next twelve months, but you were family-orientated, you enjoyed buying things for your home, and I knew you took it for granted that a husband and kids would feature in your future. I also recognised that you weren't the kind of girl to have affairs.'

'That was why you were reluctant for us to make love?'

He nodded. 'I knew you'd interpret it as a commitment. It was obvious you were as crazy about me as I was about you,' Piers continued, 'and when we slept together——' He broke off. 'Have you any idea how it felt to know I was the first? To know that such a beautiful girl, who could have had her pick of lovers, had saved herself for me? It was . . . overwhelming! If I'd needed proof of your feelings, I had it then. And then I realised that I loved you too.'

He fell silent as the steward appeared, going through the cabin, handing out blankets and drawing down the blinds. A minute or two later, the overhead lights were doused. In the rows ahead, the businessmen and the couple began to doze.

'Did you tell Barbara that I was a virgin?' Suzy asked, frowning at Piers through the gloom.

'Grief, *no*,' he protested, 'that was between you and me. I didn't even tell her your name. What I said was that I'd been seeing a girl who worked with me at *The View* and that when we'd slept together it had forced me to admit how much I cared; though I couldn't decide where things went from there. I was tempted to ask you to move in with me, but my job took me away a good eighty per cent of my time and I didn't know if it was fair when you'd have to spend so much time on your own. So I hoped that if we talked things through, Barbara might make up my mind for me.'

'Did she?'

Piers gave a dry laugh. 'No. Very wisely, she said I must decide for myself.'

'And Amanda listened to all this and so was able to produce a craftily slanted version when Dumbo here appeared,' Suzy said tightly. She covered herself up with her blanket. 'But the next time you saw me, you'd decided you didn't want us to live together.'

'No.'

'But you said you thought we were going too fast,' she protested.

'I know. You asked me once if I'd never made a complete mess of things. I did then. Boy, did I screw up! I was all set to say I loved you and suggest you move in, but at the last minute I panicked. I knew you'd regard living together as the forerunner of a permanent arrangement and, because marriage was a loaded concept, I started backing off. But when you proceeded to tell me that you'd only slept with me because you'd wanted to shed your virginity——' Piers shook a wondering head. 'Getting out of your flat without either bursting into tears or throttling you was the hardest thing I ever did. I lied,' he went on, 'I wasn't at a loose end after we split, I was devastated. For months I wanted to stand outside your house and howl. I wanted to break down your door.'

Suzy smiled at him. 'It was that bad?'

'It was purgatory!'

'You were tempted to throttle me when I turned up at the clinic,' she observed, 'and when you discovered that I'd interviewed your father.'

'True, and what made it worse was that as soon as I saw you again I knew I was still crazy about you.'

She felt a singing in her blood. 'Yes?'

'It was yet another reason—the main reason—why I asked you to move into my apartment,' Piers confessed.

'Asked?' Suzy protested. 'You didn't give me much choice.'

He grinned. 'Maybe not, but I was amazed when you agreed.'

'So was I,' she admitted. 'Did being crazy about me have anything to do with the suggestion that I should accompany you to New York?'

'It had everything to do with it,' he said. 'Likewise turning down the flat you were offered—which you then proceeded to accept. And coming on the helicopter. I persuaded Ed he ought to rest because I was jealous of the way Harv and Jason were monopolising you.'

'Jealous of two boys with galloping acne and a bizarre taste in headgear?' Suzy protested.

'Insanely. And being crazy about you is why I kept shedding my shirt,' Piers carried on. 'I figured that if I could sufficiently arouse your passions we'd end up making love—which we damn near did.'

'If we'd made love that would have solved everything?' she enquired.

'No, but it would have been a start,' he said.

Suzy looked at him. 'A start to what?'

'Spending the rest of our lives legally bound together. Once I would have been happy for us to cohabit on an open-ended basis, but over the past year I've realised that I want the same kind of things you want—a loving partner, a home, a family.' His hand covered hers. 'Will you marry me?'

The singing in her blood became a joyous chorus.

'Well——' she said, drawing out the word.

'Now I'm *very* tempted to throttle you,' Piers grinned.

Suzy laughed. 'If it's a matter of life and death— then yes.'

He leaned across the space between their seats to clasp his bandaged hand around the back of her head and draw her close.

'I've never said this to any other woman, but, Suzy, I love you. With all my heart,' he murmured, and kissed her.

It was a long kiss, a kiss which tasted and plundered her mouth, a kiss which sent her heart knocking and thudding.

'You're taking off your bandage?' she protested, when he released her and began to loosen the strapping.

'My fingers feel fine, and there's no way I'm going to make love to you one-handed.'

'I've heard about the Mile-High-Club, but you're not suggesting we make love here?' Suzy queried, as he slid his newly bared hand beneath her blanket.

'No, though I want to—heaven knows, I want to,' Piers said, secretly caressing the high curve of her breast. 'However, apart from us being arrested for disturbing the peace, you need to sleep—if you're to be bright-eyed and bushy-tailed for cancelling the move into your new flat the day after tomorrow.'

'Home at last!' Piers exclaimed, as they walked into his apartment the following morning.

Suzy grinned. 'See, you didn't expire of unrequited love.'

'But it was a close thing.'

Dropping down their suitcases, he caught hold of her and drew her into his arms. For a moment his grey eyes smiled into hers, then he began kissing her with such deep, searching kisses that her head started to spin. Sliding up beneath her shirt, he released her bra and his hands closed over the silken globes of her breasts. Suzy strained closer, and as he caressed her breasts, his fingers rubbing across the tight rigid points, a thrill of pent-up desire quivered through her. Their mutual need built and, scattering hastily shed clothes, they kissed and caressed their way into Piers' bedroom. By the time he pulled her with him on to the bed, both of them were naked.

'You have a spectacular body,' he murmured, as he gazed down at her.

'A good body,' Suzy corrected, moving forward, her breasts riding into his hands.

'Spectacular,' he insisted. 'I'm choosing the adjectives.'

She smiled at the man she loved. 'And you're spectacularly handsome,' she declared.

Slowly Piers trailed his fingers from the smoothness of her breasts, down her stomach to the furry blonde thatch between her thighs, then slowly back again.

'I want to taste you,' he said thickly, and bending his head, he covered her breast with his mouth and suckled her fiercely until wild surges of passion shuddered through her body.

'Again,' Suzy begged, in the bereft moment when he released her, and as she felt the tug of his mouth and the gentle bite of his teeth on the second swollen nipple, she writhed beneath him in unconstrained delight.

Body rubbed against body. Hair tangled with hair. Perspiration gleamed on skin. As Piers' tongue moistened her engorged nipples, the intensity of the pleasure he was giving her spiralled and her breathing quickened into sharp, rasping breaths. The hardness of him thrust against her and she was possessed by a need to touch him—there. She hesitated. Dared she? But Piers seemed to know what she was thinking, for he took hold of her hand and guided it down between their bodies.

'Darling!' Suzy breathed, as her fingers curled around him.

Piers shuddered. Once again his hand moved to her thighs, and as he caressed the tingling bud, she felt an uncontrollable shimmer of excitement and cried out. She slithered against him, again and again, until her body thrummed with sensation and she was whimpering with need.

'I love you, Sparky,' Piers murmured.

Suzy drew back. 'Why Sparky?' she asked.

'Because you're the brightest, most electric, most exciting woman I've ever met,' he vowed, and clenching the firm round curves of her buttocks, he positioned her against him and entered her.

Her head fell back on the pillow and, as he drove into her, higher and harder, Piers groaned. A compelling rhythm was established until, for one long fraught moment, he raised himself on his arms above her and was still. Loving grey eyes met loving blue. With a crazed jolt of his hips, he twitched inside her. He shuddered and moved, filling her with scalding liquid heat, and as her own climax flooded through her, she tumbled down, down, down through dark, delirious, infinite space.

CHAPTER NINE

As THE French ex-hostage whom she had profiled lengthily brought her up to date on what had been happening to him since their last meeting, Suzy sneaked yet another glance at the display table. There it was, the hardback edition of *her* book. The dark green dust-jacket bearing the title written in elegant gold letters on the front, and with a photograph of her on the back. She felt a warm glow of satisfaction. Kingdom Publishing had laid on a launch party, and to one side stood a buffet table bearing the remnants of savoury bites and tiny mouthwatering pastries, while on the other was a bar which had been dispensing glasses of vintage wine. Randolph Gardener had had his reputation as a well-known gourmet to keep up.

In his role as publisher, Randolph had also had his sales figures to think about, which meant that, after opening the evening's proceedings with a speech in which he had generously praised both her and her book, he had urged the guests to buy a copy—plus another for a friend. This many of them had done, and, for well over an hour, Suzy had been signing her name on frontispieces. But now most of the guests had departed and the evening would soon be over.

'Beautiful,' said Piers, coming up as the Frenchman finally took his leave.

Suzy looked at the greatly diminished stack of books. 'Isn't it?' she agreed.

'I meant you—in this dress, and revealing so much smooth silky flesh,' he murmured, and placing his arm around her shoulders he drew her close.

Suzy smiled up at him. After languishing in the wardrobe for more than three years, the white backless dress she had worn for the newspaper awards dinner had been taken out and dry-cleaned.

'It was you who suggested I should wear it this evening,' she reminded him, and grinned. 'Besides, I had to wear something special if I wasn't to be outclassed.'

In a charcoal grey three-piece suit, white shirt and maroon silk tie, Piers was tall and aristocratically elegant. He looked a man of gravitas, like the Political Editor he had become.

'But I never realised that seeing you dressed like this again would make me feel so damned horny,' he complained, and lowered his head.

As his mouth fastened fleetingly on the naked roundness of her shoulder, Suzy felt the moistness of his tongue, the edge of his teeth.

'Piers!' she protested, enjoying the caress and yet wary of someone else seeing.

He straightened. 'I want to bite you. I want to mark you as *mine*,' he said.

'I am yours,' she told him.

Piers smiled. 'Yes, Mrs Armstrong, you are. And as soon as we arrive home I shall peel off this tantalising dress and kiss every inch of your tantalising body and——'

'Hate to interrupt, but we must be off now,' Hugo declared, arriving beside them. He beamed at Barbara, who was holding his hand. 'We have a mountain of wedding invitations to write.'

'I hope we shall be as happy as man and wife as you two are,' Barbara whispered, as she kissed Suzy goodbye.

Suzy grinned. 'I'm sure you will be.'

'Something else to eat? Another glass of this superb wine before we end?' asked Randolph Gardener, brandishing his own glass as he bounded up beside them a minute or two later.

'No, thanks,' she said, and Piers shook his head.

'Y'know, you two getting married last month was a master stroke,' the editorial director said. 'Piers may have faded from the public mind, but your wedding turned him into a celebrity all over again. Granted, it won't last, yet even so I calculate that the interest you created should boost Suzy's sales by twenty, if not thirty, per cent.' He took a swig from his glass. 'Just a pity we couldn't have had a wedding picture of you both on the cover.'

Suzy exchanged a glance with Piers. 'Wasn't it?' she said drily.

'Sure I can't coax you to some more wine?' the *bon viveur* enquired. 'No? Well, I will,' he said, and bustled off to the bar.

'Randolph appears to think we got married simply to give your book some publicity,' Piers remarked, half an hour later, as they entered their apartment.

Suzy looked at him deadpan. 'You're not saying there were other reasons?' she demanded.

'I am.' He placed his arm around her waist. 'And if you'd care to come into the bedroom right now, I'll demonstrate one of them.'

She grinned. 'Yessir!'

'You know what I find so amazing?' he said, as he drew her down on to the bed. 'The way, after being so damned argumentative, you've discovered a consuming passion for meeting my every whim.'

'It's a two-way thing,' Suzy protested.

Piers smiled a tender smile. 'It is, my love,' he said. 'It is.'